THE ANGEL OF DARKNESS

MICHAEL MCGEE

www.darkmythpublications.com/

> The sale of this book without its cover is unauthorized. If you purchased this book without a cover, you should be aware that it was reported to the publisher as "unsold and destroyed." Neither the author nor the publisher has received payment for the sale of this "stripped book."

This book is a work of fiction. Names, characters, places, and incidents are products of the author's imagination or are used fictitiously. Any resemblance to actual events or locales or persons, living or dead, is entirely coincidental.

Dark Myth Publications, a division of
The JayZoMon Dark Myth Company, LLC.
21050 Little Beaver Rd, Apple Valley, CA 92308

Copyright 2023 by Michael McGee
Cover Art by Rebecca McGee

All rights reserved, including the right to reproduce this book or portions thereof in any form whatsoever.
For information address, 21050 Little Beaver Rd, Apple Valley, Ca 92308

ISBN: 979-8-9863807-6-6

First Printing April 2023

Dark Myth Publications is a registered trademark of The JayZoMon Dark Myth Company, LLC.

10 9 8 7 6 5 4 3 2 1

Table of Contents

Introduction………..........…........................xi

Prologue...01
Chapter One...05
Chapter Two...19
Chapter Three..39
Chapter Four..49
Chapter Five...59
Chapter Six...69
Chapter Seven...81
Chapter Eight...93
Chapter Nine..105
Chapter Ten..113
Chapter Eleven..131
Chapter Twelve..145
Chapter Thirteen..163
Chapter Fourteen...177
Chapter Fifteen..189
Chapter Sixteen...201
Chapter Seventeen...209
Chapter Eighteen...219
Epilogue..227

About the Author………..........…..................229

*For my family who supported me.
My sister, Rebecca, for her amazing artwork talent.
My fellow writers who gave me helpful feedback.
To Dani and Steve Alcorn who's writing classes helped me improve my craft.
Stephanie Bardy for being a very dedicated, and patient, editor.
Writer, Chris Bice, for introducing me to the great people at Dark Myth Publications.*

Introduction

I wrote this story in pieces, often writing sections far ahead of where I was currently in the plot segments, while in university learning how to become a police officer. This story came about thanks to inspiration from the video game "Smite" and a song which shares the same name as this tale.

Michael McGee
February, 2023

THE ANGEL OF DARKNESS

Prologue

THE BIG THREE sat in their throne room on Olympus, all questioning a mysterious force they felt moments ago. Rivers of uncertainty shot down their spines when they experienced the rush of fear. Zeus was the first to speak.

"We all felt it; a disturbance in the balance of nature."

"Yes, I felt it down in the Underworld," spoke the God of death, Hades. "The dead were stirred in their eternal sleep."

"The creatures of the deep could feel ripples in the water though the oceans were as calm as glass," spoke the sea God, Poseidon.

The three Gods pondered at the source of this occurrence. Then Zeus had an idea. It was only an act that the Gods took if they were in desperate need for an answer to questions they could not find.

"We should consult the waters of the Ancients. They have gifted us with enlightenment before; they may be able to do it again."

Hades and Poseidon both pondered this idea. The waters were crafted by The Ancients, great beings who came before the Gods. They were the ones who saw all. Saw the future and past collide in a fury of events that became known as the present. They were wise and powerful. If anyone had the answer, it was them.

The three Gods took a long journey down to the deepest corridor of Olympus. They had placed several traps to safeguard their secrets, only they as the strongest of the Olympians could pass through them. Zeus absorbed lighting so powerful that one blast could send an entire civilization into ruin. Poseidon calmed waters of such fury that anything caught in the current would drown within seconds. Hades banished spirits which would cause endless pain and suffering beyond death to anyone, even a God, who encountered them.

With their barriers disabled, the Gods reached their destination. A basin of water held by an ancient statue that no one ever dared to even scratch. Its beauty was unlike anything anyone had ever seen. An ancient being whom no-one knew the identity of. As the Gods reached the basin they looked at each other in unison. Together they dipped their heads beneath the surface. Spirits lifted from bodies as the Gods were shown their own fate.

Zeus saw a sky of beauty, lighted by the brightest sun which shined brilliantly. As he stared, he caught a glimpse of a shadow passing over the sky. It became dark; night had fallen in the early afternoon of a perfect day. A faint laugh passed over the land. A laugh that haunted Zeus beyond measure.

Poseidon saw the seas of the world become mist as a powerful blue flame erupted upon the surface. No wave that was summoned nor storm that was generated could extinguish the burning sea. The creatures of the deep fell as the God of the sea watched in horror, unable to save them.

Hades saw a figure in the Underworld. A figure with skin fainter than bone, wielding a sword of light. Hades summoned creatures of death to banish this intruder from his land. One swing of the sword obliterated all opposing forces. The unknown person drew back its blade as it disappeared. Not a moment later, Hades felt something pierce his body. The intruder had rushed towards him faster than anything Hades could see and struck its blade within his chest. The light of the blade burning his body like nothing he'd ever felt before. Hades felt his own existence fade away into the darkness of the Underworld, as the intruder glanced at him with an evil smile.

Hades' spirit reconnected with his body as he screamed in pain. Unable to breath, he threw his body from the waters of the basin. He landed on the floor, his breathing heavy with fear, Hades glanced at his brothers, both turned to him with stunned horror across their faces. They had all seen something within the waters, something dark, and evil. The Gods sat on the floor; the answer they were seeking only replaced by new questions. How was this going to happen? When was it to occur? Who was the one responsible? Was this their true fate?

Chapter One

IT WAS A bright morning in the town of Mountainegra. The sun was red as it rose into the blue sky. No one knew why the morning brought such brilliant colors. They just admired it every day. Everyone in both the worlds above and below could feel new and free as each new day began. It was a world of pleasure and peace for everyone. Everyone that is, except Yuko who was currently running for her life.

Where she was running to she did not know. What she was running from she did not know either. All she knew was that something was chasing her, and she had to run. Turning around she saw darkness, before her she saw darkness, darkness surrounded her on all sides. She then heard a piercing sound behind her. Turning around she saw something white jump from the shadows, then she felt pain, sharp pain around her neck and on her chest. She screamed weakly, trying to call for help. Whatever was grabbing her neck suddenly released it, taking the opening Yuko screamed again.

"Aaaahhh!"

The dream was like nothing she'd ever felt before. She'd had nightmares in the past as all humans did, but this was different. It felt different. Usually, nightmares were something you could just wake up from and they would be over, the mental pain would subside. This time however felt physical. It had felt as if her body had been torn apart, sweat covered her body and her arms and legs were stiff. She sat there for a moment resting and letting the pain fade. Yuko assumed she had just slept in an odd position. It was a new bed after all.

First night in her family's new home, in their new town. Yuko and her family had moved to this new town near the Rocky Mountains within the western side of Canada. Coming here from Japan was an experience for the young girl. Her father worked for an automotive company. Due to a lack in being unable to keep up with the rest of the world in technological advances, the company began suffering communication issues. Orders would take between several weeks to a month to reach the Canadian borders. As such the company decided to relocate several of their highest representatives to Canada so they could receive plans before production began. Yuko's father was one of the chief designers of the company and he knew that finding more work to support his family would have been extremely difficult. So, he and his family had to move across the

ANGEL OF DARKNESS

Pacific Ocean to a new world to help sustain their lives. No one in the family was particularly pleased with this act, but to keep their family healthy and together, they had no other choice. Coming to Canada was scary at first, as was all new journeys.

There was a knock on her bedroom door. "Yuko, are you alright?" It was her mother.

"Yes, I'm fine, just had an odd dream that's all."

"Again, this is the third one this month, are you sure you're alright?"

"It's fine mom, I'm just a little shaken from the long flight yesterday."

"Alright, well breakfast is ready for you when you come downstairs."

"Thanks, I'll be down in a minute."

Moving from under her covers Yuko stretched her legs as she sat up on her bed. The morning sun shone through her window, the rays being stopped by her blinds, but shining through the opening between them. Her room was a bit of a mess, but they had just moved in so some organization would be required.

Standing up Yuko walked over to her desk and moved through the objects. Her CDs were from her favorite music artists; the rock and rolling Green Day, the smooth, calm, Johnathan Morali, and the country king, in her opinion, Keith Urban. She never could explain her reasons for enjoying music from the English language rather than her native Japanese tongue. But to those few people who questioned her about it, she would simply reply, "Well I enjoy it. It makes me calm and lets me relax after a stressful day." Somehow that always satisfied the curiosity of those who bothered to ask her about the kind of music she enjoyed, so she stuck with it. She did however have albums from the Japanese music stars LiSA and Garnidelia, as well as some burned CDs from the vocaloid pop star Hatsune Miku, those artists always managed to make her smile.

There were photos were of her and her friends underneath all sorts of things, from cherry blossom trees to the Nijo Castle. She already missed her friends, but she knew she would make new ones here in Canada, so she stayed herself and smiled. Her books were of Japanese literature, some famous artists overseas that Yuko always enjoyed reading. Her laptop didn't have anything special on it, old files that weren't any use anymore.

Should probably get rid of that stuff, Yuko told herself. Her camera was new, nothing fancy or hi-tech just a plain old instant film-based camera she used to take photos of whatever she saw that made her smile or was just a moment she wanted to capture forever. Usually that meant one of her friends sitting on a park bench with the sunset in the background, a perfect shot every time. Her backpack lay on the floor beside her desk, it didn't have anything in it except some pencils and paper for drawing or writing her thoughts down.

Yuko walked out of her room and headed for the bathroom. A morning shower always felt good and thankfully this house had running water where you could adjust the temperature. Cold water just never felt good on skin, it made people cold and miserable, warm water was always what Yuko preferred. Shutting the door behind her Yuko looked at herself in the mirror. A simple girl from Japan with jet black hair looked back at her with a face that looked like a zombie. A face that made her smile as it was a look that most people woke up to in the morning. Turning on the water and shedding her clothes she stepped into the shower, the warm water instantly taking its effects on her body. Loosening up her tense muscles and aching head, that dream still haunted her even though it was over, it just felt like something more. She decided not to worry about it too much and just try to enjoy the day. Washing up her body and shutting off the water, Yuko stepped out of the shower and looked back at herself in the mirror once again. Her reflection smiled back at her.

This is how I want to be, always.

Yuko left the bathroom and walked to her bedroom to get changed. She never wore anything flashy or stylish; she was always simple with her clothes. She opened her closet and wondered, staring at her hangers. She decided to go with a simple look, red shirt with a grey hoodie and dark blue jeans. Something simple that reflected her innocence in the world, and it wouldn't make her stand out as a new student in her new school. Going down to breakfast, Yuko could smell the sweetness that was in the kitchen.

"Morning mom." she said as she sat down.

"Morning sweetie, I made waffles for breakfast, thought it would be simple and easy for the first day in our new home, and it might be nice to try some of the food from this country."

"You're the best," Yuko replied as her mother brought over a plate with three golden wheels of wheat. The store they visited the previous day to get some provisions didn't have much food from Japan, so they had to take food from the culture of their new country which the family was fine with as it was what they had available to them and were also tired from the long trip.

"What's that?" Yuko asked, noticing a plastic bottle on the table.

"Maple syrup, I heard from the locals that it's the best in the world over here as this is where they produce it from the maple trees in this area, go ahead and try it," her mother said.

Pouring some over in the corner of the plate, Yuko picked up her fork, which felt odd because she always ate with chopsticks, so her muscle memory wasn't in tune with the shape, Stabbing one of the pieces of gold, she dipped it into the sugar turning the gold into an odd muddy color; it wasn't pleasant. Taking the first bite however, Yuko's face lit up. The syrup was sweeter than she expected, and the taste exploded in her mouth.

"Woah, Yuko what are you doing?" Her mother asked as she almost drowned her waffles in the sweetness from the bottle. Finishing up Yuko kissed her mother once, grabbed her bento off the table, and headed out to catch the bus. Thankfully, the school had mailed a map of all the bus routes around the town, so she knew where to wait. The school bus came on time and Yuko hopped on.

Alright, time for an awesome day.

While all this was occurring in the land of humans; above the clouds, where light always shone, in a kingdom of pillars and statues known to the humans as Olympus; Zeus the king of the Gods stretched his arms as he prepared for his morning battle practice. Over two thousand years had passed since he and his brothers witnessed the images within the ancient waters. Though many of the Gods in

ANGEL OF DARKNESS

Olympus began to forget about what they were told when the three returned from the chamber, Zeus was not easily accepting of the low possibility of this force rising up against him and the other Gods of his domain; for no matter how close to zero the possibility may be it still exists.

Zeus knew this and was going to be ready for anything. Ares, the God of war, was always ready for a fight, he was always prepared for battle and his chains of binding were always strong. He had agreed to help Zeus in his combat training and tactics, then in case an enemy did rise; he would be ready. For over two millennia Ares had set up traps and battled against his father almost every day. Each challenge became more and more difficult. Zeus had to summon lightning storms and cast lightning from his fingers at once to stop the forces that approached him, a task that took every ounce of his strength, but soon became no more strength than required to lift a finger.

Today, Ares had taken the day to rest, so Zeus had set up targets which would appear at random. Which he would have to strike down within seconds to succeed. Calling lightning to his hands, he prepared for the first target. It rose several meters to his left, with a back throw the lightning traveled over the clouds and struck the target dead center. Three targets followed these were armed with bow and arrows, Zeus shot several bolts towards them, simply strafing to the side was enough for the targets to avoid them.

"Blast! Ares sure didn't make this simple," Zeus chuckled he knew the God of war never made things easy. As the targets reappeared, Zeus tried a different tactic, summoning a storm above the targets he dispatched one of them with ease, the second and third fired their bows straight at the God's head. Zeus held up his shield to deflect the arrows and retaliated with a stream of lightning within the clouds below the targets, vaporizing them from below.

"Well fired, God of all heavens."

Alarmed, Zeus turned around to face the source of the voice, a bolt of lightning clutched in his fist. A raven stood on a statue, one that was black and blue with eyes that glimmered like stars deep within the galaxy. Zeus's face changed to one of simplicity.

"Hugin, one of the two ravens who serve as the eyes and ears of the Norse king, Odin" Zeus said with a small smile.

"It's been a while, great one" replied the bird "Your biceps look as strong as ever."

"Ares knows how to strengthen even the weakest of warriors; he can turn a man of skin and bone into a warrior entire armies would fear."

"He cannot, however, strengthen a feathered creature such as I" sighed the raven, cleaning his wings.

"True, so what brings you to my domain?" the sky God asked, taking a seat on the clouds.

"A gathering of Gods is to be held soon, Lord Odin requests your presence and that of your brothers on a matter you once faced long ago." The raven answered with a glow in his eyes.

"What matter is it they wish to discuss?"

"I know not, I'm told by Lord Odin that I must ask you and your brother's attend; nothing more was to be spoken on this day about this event."

"Very well, I will consult my brothers on this matter and

see that we are all there."

"When you are ready, simply use this," the raven picked at his right wing until he turned towards the God, a small crystal in its beak, it shined like the waters of the sea. The raven dropped the blue stone into the outstretched hand of the thunder king. "This gem will instantly teleport you to Asgard, the meeting will begin in three full sun rotations."

"I will ensure we are present." Zeus replied as he stared at the gem.

The raven nodded and with one squawk from his beak disappeared in a cloud of smoke.

Below the waves of the Pacific Ocean the sea God, Poseidon, sat on his throne atop a mountain of coral. Seaweed danced in the water's current as sea creatures swam across the ocean floor. Several dolphins swam past the sea God, mermaids alongside them. They waved to their king who waved back with a calm smile. A pike chased clownfish around the bay; they easily eluded the predator within the anemones surrounding the coral reefs. Poseidon didn't bother to disturb them as the way of nature, where everything eats everything else, was a natural order that even the ruler of the seven seas couldn't fight against. Nature always won that fight and it was pointless to try and battle with what you couldn't control.

As the sea God rose from his throne to go for a walk, he felt a sudden presence approach. Gripping his trident, he prepared a flurry of water in case it was an attack. A bolt of lightning crashed down upon the sea floor; waves rolled around the area as a figure rose from the singed ground. None of the sea creatures in the area were harmed, they stared as the figure before them rose. Recognizing the one who struck their home; the sea turned to its ruler, Poseidon's expression changed from alarm to anger like the crash of a wave on the land above.

"Zeus, how many times do I have to tell you to not enter my domain that way?!!"

"Oh brother, you know I never come down to bring harm to those around you, the lightning that teleports me down here is as weak as the electricity that flows through your body as we speak."

Poseidon simply stared at his brother for a second, before bursting into a hardy laughter.

"Hahaha, well it's good to see you brother. How are things in the sky?"

"Oh, you know, light during the day and mysterious during the night, I simply control the weather for the mortals of earth. What do you want me to do?"

"I don't know; cause chaos with a storm every now and then?"

"You know I refuse to cause extreme damage to those who fuel our power. Their belief gives us strength."

"True, so why have you come down here at this time?"

"Hugin, the raven from the North came to me with a message, there is to be a meeting held in three days' time about an event that myself, you, and our brother Hades are acquainted with, and we three have been summoned."

"Many events have occurred over the years, I'm curious as to which event it is that they wish to discuss with us."

"I wonder that myself, which is why I believe it would be wise for us to attend, will you travel with me?"

ANGEL OF DARKNESS

"The seas have been pretty calm these last few years, I believe a few days away won't be a problem, count me in."

"I am pleased to hear that, now I must travel to the Underworld and ask the same from Hades." With a flash, Zeus vanished in a spark of light, a patch of red sand sat on the ocean floor before the chill of the waters calmed it once more.

Hades had never been the most reasonable God, having been betrayed by his brothers into becoming the lord of the dead was not what the God had originally intended for himself. Through time Hades grew accustomed to life in the valley of the dead. Flames rising out pits of eternal suffering and pain. Often Hades would travel to the surface to gaze upon the land of the living; he enjoyed it, twisting something minor to gain some entertainment at the pain of the humans. He had already released his wife, Persephone, back to Olympus for the summer months, which was his agreement with Zeus after he forced the Goddess of beauty to marry him. For her beauty was beyond what the God of the dead could ever imagine.

Now he was pacing back and forth along a river of souls, wondering when something would happen that would end his newly acquired boredom. A loud barking suddenly echoed through the caverns, shaking the walls.

"Cerberus!!" Yelled the God in rage as his dog's barks rang through the corridors.

Freeing his soul from his body, Hades glided over the river towards the gates of the Underworld, and towards the shattering outbursts from his guardian companion. As he approached, his body returning to him, he stood behind his dog trying to look at what had steered Cerberus on this surprisingly calm day. As one of Cerberus's heads turned towards his master, Hades was able to look past the flaming maw of the beast at who was beyond the gate to the Underworld. Surprise hit his face as there, with two of Cerberus's heads facing him, stood his brother Zeus.

"Zeus, what are you doing here in the Underworld?"

"Would you mind getting this slobbering mutt to leave me alone first, my robes are already singed to hell."

"Down Cerberus!"

The dog obeyed and retreated down the corridor. Hades raised his finger and the gates to the city of the dead creaked open.

"What brings you to my realm?"

"First, when did you get this gate? My teleportation powers were halted by its aura, when I tried to phase through I was blocked by a barrier, and then that guard dog of yours showed up and began spitting fire at me."

"I crafted that a while ago to ensure no one like your son Hercules would sneak his way into my domain again, even Charon my boatman needs to wait for Cerberus's word before passing through here."

"Ah, well as you know he was trying to save many lives and needed some of your power to do so."

"True, he could have just asked me first by talking to Charon about talking to me. But now back to present matters, why have you come here?"

"There is to be a meeting in three days at Asgard, we have been asked to attend."

"The home of that old man who claims to guard many

worlds but can't even control his own son from running off with his hammer? Ha-ha."

"Odin may be old, but he is still extremely wise, it might be best to see what he has to say. You weren't doing anything during this season anyway, not with Persephone out of the picture."

"I was hoping you wouldn't bring her up, but at the same time you are right. I have been rather bored these last few weeks; no one of interest has died recently. When and where do we depart?"

"The gates of Olympus at first light three days from today."

"I'll be there." The God of Death replied in a foul voice as Cerberus growled from around the corner as some trapped souls tried to escape.

Chapter Two

THE BUS DROVE on down the road at a steady speed. Stopping at several houses to pick up other students. Most of whom seemed to know each other. No one seemed to notice the girl sitting in the rear of the bus, too caught up in their conversations about summer and sports that they were oblivious of her presence. Yuko didn't really mind; she knew it would take a while before anyone noticed her. As the bus pulled up to a red house on the street corner Yuko looked out the window, she stared out into the sun as the girl who the bus stopped for ran up to it from the front door. A young girl, about Yuko's age, wearing dark clothes and had aqua blue hair. Yuko could see small specks of dark hair on the sides of this girl's head, she assumed that was her true color, it looked like she was a brunette.

For some reason Yuko couldn't take her eyes off her. Most of the other students had blonde or dark hair, she however seemed to dislike her current color and so covered it over with a new color. It intrigued Yuko as she stared through the window. Like the other students who jumped on the bus, this girl hopped on and began walking towards the back of the bus, head down, scanning for an empty seat. Taking a seat across from Yuko, the girl looked out the window, did not speak, and appeared to drift off into thought. Yuko turned back to the window as well, not wanting to disturb her.

The bus drove on for another ten minutes until it pulled up to the town's high school. The students at the front quickly filed out towards the school. When Yuko got off the bus she walked off to the side and looked at the building. It was old, made of brick and only had 2 floors. There was a flagpole where the Canadian flag was waving in the light breeze. Yuko walked inside and looked around.

The entryway was very open and circular. Several hallways extend from opposite ends of the building leading down to hallways covered in metal lockers and doors leading to classrooms. A stairwell stood across from the entrance where students were climbing up to the second floor of the building, down other hallways and towards other classrooms. Yuko looked around, unsure as to where the main office was. Soon she spotted it to her left, a door with the word "office" painted over the glass. Yuko stepped inside; no one was at the front desk, so she decided to take a seat. Several minutes passed, Yuko simply looked out the window behind her; watching other students walking through the school. A door opened behind her, but she didn't notice as her mind was lost in thought.

"Can I help you?"

Yuko jumped in her seat as the voice brought her mind back to her body. She quickly turned around and stared back at the middle-aged woman who looked surprised by her reaction.

"Are you alright?" the woman asked.

"Um… yes, I'm fine, sorry lost myself there," Yuko replied as she stood up.

"Oh, that's alright I do that myself, how can I help you?" the woman asked, taking a seat behind the desk in the center of the room.

"Well, um… My name is Yuko, Yuko Asami. I just moved here with my parents from Japan and I'm joining this school today."

"Nice to meet you Yuko, I'm Mrs. Faye. Principal of this school. Let me just check to see where you are in my files." Mrs. Faye opened a drawer of her desk and brought out a file folder, Yuko saw on the folder was labeled "Students A-H." After flipping through several sheets of paper Mrs. Faye pulled out a small set of papers and placed them on her desk.

"Alright, let's see." Mrs. Faye said as she closed the student folder. Yuko moved her seat closer as the principal turned the file around for her to see. Her name was on the top with her date of birth underneath it. Following that was the school's name, "Mountainegra High School," and her scheduled classes succeeding that.

Yuko had already received a copy of her class list; she brought it with her just in case she needed a reminder as to which rooms her classes were in. Her classes were the same on her sheet as the ones on the copy the principle retrieved from her folder. English 10, Science 10, Physical Education 15, Social Studies 10, Mathematics 10, and Industrial Arts 10. The physical education class and the construction were options that were not a part of the Alberta curriculum, so she didn't need them to graduate high school. Yuko decided that they would be good classes where she could try new things and have fun at the same time.

"Are those the correct classes you wish to take?"

"Yes, those are the right ones."

"Alright do you have any ques-" she began before the door opened. "Oh; hello Max."

Yuko turned around and saw the blue haired girl she had seen on the bus.

Max, I wonder why she is named that.

Max took a seat behind Yuko and looked towards her; a face glared at her. Yuko turned away.

"Sorry, please finish up." Max said with a still expression.

"Thank you, so Yuko did you have any questions about anything?" Mrs. Faye asked, returning her attention to the girl before her.

"Um... Is there anyone I could follow around for help in finding all the classrooms for the classes I'm taking?"

"Well as luck would have it Max here is taking the same courses you are, maybe she would be willing to help you."

"Would that be alright with you Max; sorry can I call you that?"

ANGEL OF DARKNESS

Max turned around as she had been staring out the window into the sky; "What was that?"

"I was wondering if you would be able to help me find my classes." Yuko asked her.

"Sure, why not," she said with a small grunt.

Yuko turned around, slightly annoyed by that grunt but decided to let it slide. "Thank you for the help this morning." She said to the principle followed by a bow.

"You're welcome and please come back anytime you need to see me."

Yuko straightened up and went outside to wait by the door for Max. As soon as the door closed Yuko let out a large sigh. "That was more stressful than I thought."

Another five minutes passed before the office door opened and Max came stepping out, she held a set of notes in her hand.

"What's that?" Yuko asked curiously.

"A note telling the teacher why we are late to class, and a reminder for me about something I did, but that's not your problem so don't worry about it." Max said that last bit sharply, it kind of scared Yuko. "Anyway, my name's Max, you found that out easily back in the office, what's your name?"

"Yuko."

"What class do you have first?"

Yuko looked at her class list and found the class based on what the time was; currently it was 9:25. "I have math 10, room 215."

"Ok I've got that same class too; it's on the second floor,

this way." Max walked off towards the opposite end of the central area of the school Yuko followed behind. "The way this school's rooms work is that there is a number in front of every room number that indicates which floor it's on." Yuko looked back at her form and saw the number 2 in front of 'room 215', which had eluded her before, so she was thankful Max had pointed it out.

"Oh, thanks I didn't see that before."

"Don't mention it."

As they reached the top of the stairs Yuko saw two hallways leading out to different areas of the building, she asked which one they needed to take.

"Well, they both loop around and meet back here, the rooms expand around the loop and go in order from lowest number to the highest beginning down this first hallway here." Max indicated the hallway closest to their position at the foot of the stairwell. "It's designed so that people don't need to loop all the way around to get to their classes if they're in the higher room numbers. But most people ignore that simple way and crowd around this first entryway, my advice is to wait in the back until the mess has cleared up and then move into the hallway. As for room 215 it's at the end of this hallway on the right."

Yuko followed Max down the hallway as she began to stroll down the labyrinth of lockers. While they walked Yuko noted the room numbers as they passed: 208, 209, and 210, it followed that pattern for several more rooms and sections of lockers until the two reached the room labeled 215 around the corner on the right side of the hallway. Max opened the door to the classroom and walked in casually, Yuko on the other hand simply peaked in to get a look at the class.

The room was small; only about twenty desks were inside; small bookshelves sat on the far side of the room underneath the windows. The wall adjacent to the door held a posting board with several sections separated by a yellow band of tape. The sections were labelled at the top of each row: Math 10, Math 20, and Math 30 each one in vivid green, red, and blue letters. A desk sat in the corner of the room with papers resting on the surface, next to a computer. Behind the desk stood a green filing cabinet with several drawers; again, each was labelled with the classes' grade level.

It just looked like a regular classroom; Yuko didn't really expect too much difference here as the school rooms in Japan were fairly basic as well. There were about twelve students already sitting at their desks, pencils in hand with notebooks in front of them. Several of them stopped writing and looked at Yuko as she stared into the room. Yuko's anxiety rose, her heart began beating furiously. She saw Max walk up the front of the room where the teacher was standing, after she handed the teacher the note from the principle; she swiftly strolled off to a desk in the back of the room near the back window and sat down, looking tired and slightly miserable. The teacher looked down at the note, then towards Yuko in the doorway.

"Hello, are you Yuko?"

"Yes." Yuko replied as the class turned towards her.

"Well, Yuko there's a seat behind Max there on the left side of the room if you'd like to sit there."

"Thanks." Yuko said as she walked over to the back of the room to the empty desk. Max was still staring out the window; a few of the students turned back to the teacher while others were still glancing at Yuko through the corner of their eyes.

The class was pretty simple, being that it was the first day of classes a slow easy day was expected. The teacher simply handed out a small test; which she said was for information on how much each student remembered about past mathematical equations. Yuko found it pretty easy; most of the questions were simple and easy to decipher. When the bell rang most of the students funneled out into the halls, Yuko stayed behind and waited for Max.

"So how was that quiz for you?" She asked Max when they walked out of the room.

"I never really put too much effort into those things." Max replied. "I have construction class next, what about you?"

Yuko scanned her class list, "Same."

"That's cool" Max replied in a dull voice. Yuko looked at her, wondering what was wrong, she seemed down ever since the day began. "Well, we don't want to be late," She said as she began down the hall, Yuko ran to catch up to her.

The construction classroom was on the lower floor in the corner near one of the emergency exits to the school.

"It's the only place where they can get the pipes for the dust collection vents." Max told Yuko as she sagged into the room.

The class was slightly larger than her previous one; about 30 students. Desks were spread out over the room. The shop area could be seen behind a wall of glass and a closed door on the opposite side of the room. Most of the students were already engaged in conversations about what the class would be like; obviously, they were eager to start building things. The teacher walked in and took attendance after the bell rang. He noticed Yuko sitting in the middle of the room halfway through.

"Hello, who are you?"

"I'm Yuko Asami, I'm joining this school today."

"Oh, you're Yuko, Mrs. Faye told me you'd be joining us today. Glad to meet you, I'm Mr. Johnson."

"Nice to meet you as well."

The class went rather smoothly; Mr. Johnson told the class that they would not be entering the shop to begin constructing objects until about three weeks from today. Most of the class got upset as they were eager to begin the fun part of the course. The rest seemed to understand the value of safety. Some of the machines that Yuko saw behind the glass in the other room did look dangerous if not handled correctly. A few of them had the blade exposed from below the cutting surface while others had the blade above the cutting area. Yuko had never handled some of the machines within the shop before so she knew that learning how to properly handle those devices was necessary before the fun could begin.

Looking beside her Yuko noticed that Max was engaged in this class. Her eyes were following the teacher rather than staring at her desk or out a window, which was not an option in this room because there were no windows, but Max appeared interested in what they were doing. It made Yuko happy to see that Max seemed to have a content way about her rather than the quiet way she was first introduced to.

When the bell rang for lunch most of the class rocketed out of the room, Max however walked towards Mr. Johnson and began chatting with him. Yuko was busy looking at the tools through the window that she didn't notice. When she turned around Max was heading for the door.

"Did you have a question you wanted to ask me?" Mr. Johnson asked.

"Oh, no I think I'm ok." Yuko began walking towards the door before a thought struck her. "Actually, I was wondering why that table has a blade exposed through its base?" She asked, turning around.

"Have you ever seen a table saw before?" Mr. Johnson asked.

"No, I haven't."

"Well, it's normally protected by a blade guard that prevents the fingers or other objects such as jewelry and long hair from being caught within the blade's motion. The guard was removed yesterday because I needed the extra room to cut a thicker piece of wood for a shed I'm currently working on for a friend of mine for his cabin. The downside to using the blade guard is that you can't raise the blade very high and make it possible to cut larger pieces."

"It must be pretty dangerous to remove the guard."

"Yes, it is very dangerous however when used properly and safely it's sometimes alright to remove the guard. We won't be removing it however as most of the pieces we will need to cut won't be that thick."

"Thanks for the information," Yuko replied before heading out the door.

ANGEL OF DARKNESS

Yuko couldn't see Max anywhere outside the classroom, so she decided to follow some students who were exiting into the hall from the adjacent rooms. They headed into the core where many students were getting lunch from the cafeteria. Yuko spotted Max near the rear of the line. Yuko went and grabbed a table near the back of the core opposite the main entrance. Two empty seats were beside her and she decided to hold one for Max. Grabbing her bento from her bag Yuko looked around at some of the other tables.

Most of the students were in fast conversations with one another. Some of them were playing a card game of sorts surrounded by observers watching their game. Other students were on their phones and not paying attention to anything around them; Yuko never really understood the use of phones and electronic devices during eating times. In Japan she always sat and talked with her family during mealtimes. She was told to take her electronic devices and keep them in her room, it was considered more polite. Her father even turned off his computer so that he couldn't get interrupted by emails from his boss who usually always contacted the family during dinner time. As she grabbed a hold of the chopsticks that were in her lunch bag Yuko was approached by three girls.

"Hey, you're new here aren't you?" A tall blonde one asked.

"Yes, I am," Yuko replied. "I'm Yuko it's nice to meet you."

"Yeah, whatever, so when are you going to move?" a red-haired girl asked in a stern voice.

"I'm sorry what do you mean?"

"From this spot, this is our table." the blonde one replied.

MICHAEL MCGEE

"Your table?" Yuko asked curiously.

"Yes we always sit here, and the entire school knows it, we own this school so we can do whatever we want, and this here is our spot during this hour so move it before we have to use other methods to make you move," the third girl said sternly. She was very tall and leered over Yuko while she said that.

Yuko wasn't sure what to do. She never was one to pick fights and she certainly did not want to start one now on the first day. As she looked back at the three girls who were all glaring at her someone placed a hand on the tall blonde one from behind.

"Hey, don't touch me you creep!" The blonde girl cried as she spun around with a nasty look on her face. Yuko saw Max standing there facing the blonde girl, her hand was on the girl's shoulder, and she looked pretty angry. The other two girls turned around and Yuko saw that they swiftly became frightened.

"What are you three doing?" Max asked quietly, not taking her eyes off her captive.

"We were about to teach this new girl how things are done around here, you don't have a problem with that, do you little Miss Trouble Child?"

Trouble child? Yuko wondered.

"No, but I was wondering why you were picking on a new girl, that's not usually your style of victim. Usually, I see you going after the toughest of the students here, Little Miss Queen of the Grounds." Max replied staring into her face with a face that showed anger.

Yuko began to worry that things were about to escalate

for everyone around them when someone yelled out from behind the five of them.

"Hey, what seems to be the problem here."

The five girls all turned around to the face of a uniformed male who looked pretty upset about the situation. Max released the girl and turned around to face the man.

"Nothing, just having a little argument about an event that happened this morning on the bus." Max replied quickly.

"Well, let's try and keep it under control." The uniformed man said sternly. "We don't want any trouble going on in this school you know that."

"Sorry sir." The blonde lady said as she and the other two scattered leaving only Max and Yuko in the heat zone. The man left and Max turned to face Yuko who was staring back at her with a hint of humor.

"What's with that smirk?"

"I don't know that was really awesome of you."

"That was nothing, you might want to stay away from those three, they're not the friendliest people."

"Who are they?"

"They're the gang the rest of the students call 'The Sisters' and that's not because they are girls." Max said taking a seat beside Yuko, her lunch was a burger and a bottle of water which she held in her free hand on a tray.

"Why are they called 'The Sisters'?"

"Because they act like they rule the school and act like they are cool when they're really not. Half this school tries to act cool and fit in with them; most of the time they fail miserably."

"What about you?"

"What do you mean?"

"That girl, I'm guessing she's the leader, called you the "Trouble Child". What was that all about?"

"That girl's name is Victoria, she's a total snake and so are the other two. The redhead is named Ashly and she is not a friendly person at all, some say she was born rude. As for the black haired one her name is Mandy; she loves to pick fights on smaller people simply because she is tall and can leer over them. As for that name they called me; I wouldn't worry about it, it's my problem and not yours."

"How do you know them?"

"They went to the same school as me prior to joining this school. Their reputation had just started when I was in grade nine. Most of the students here attended the same school previously; so, the Sisters have more influence over them; which is why everyone avoids them."

The two girls ate in silence for a while before Yuko got curious about Max. She got curious about her name, it seemed like it was a nickname, but she could not figure out what it was. Her curiosity got the better of her.

"Hey, can I ask you something?"

"What is it?" Max replied.

"On the topic of people's names, I was wondering what your name was. I mean Max seems like a nickname for a larger name, but I don't know what it would be. What is it short for?"

ANGEL OF DARKNESS

Max stared at Yuko for a minute. Yuko wasn't sure if she'd been too forward or too curious, maybe she should have just minded her own business. Yuko turned away.

"My name is Maxine." Max said quietly.

Yuko looked back up at her. "Maxine, that's a nice name."

"Thanks, but I prefer Max."

"Alright Max." Yuko replied with a small smile.

The rest of the day went rather well for Max and Yuko. The Sisters were not in any of their classes which was a relief for Yuko. The science class went smoothly. Max stared at her notes all class and kept quiet. Yuko listened to the teacher talk about what they would be going over during the semester; the only subset of the course that Yuko thought would be the problem for her was physics. She didn't have the best memory and some of the conversions looked difficult. The teacher, Mr. Smith, told her it would not be very difficult within this level of physics they would be taught. This calmed Yuko's nerves a bit.

The final class of the day was physical education, most students called it gym. This class, like the previous three, went smoothly. The class consisted of a mix of male and female students, and we're all given lockers to hold their personal items as well as gym clothes. Once the class returned from the dressing rooms the teacher set them into two groups for a simple game of dodgeball, he said that because it was the first day they wouldn't need to go into the curriculum right away and would start tomorrow.

Yuko and Max were placed on opposite teams and while Yuko was fast on the court; Max was flexible. She barely moved and yet dodged almost every ball fired at her, almost; except for the curveball one student threw at her from the side. Yuko's speed made her a tricky target to hit but the rest of the class was tired from the long first day and so didn't put up much of a fight. She was able to knock out two girls and three boys before getting knocked out herself. Thankfully, the final member of her team managed to knock his opponent to the ground easily, sealing a win. When the clock read quarter to three the teacher called everyone in for final announcements which were basically a simple 'have a good day speech' and the class was dismissed to the locker rooms.

After the class left; most of the students headed for the bus to go home for the night. Max said she was going to head home as well as she had family business she had to help with. Yuko decided to head home also for she was tired from the day. They sat beside each other on the bus. Max remained quiet for the trip. Yuko silently stared out the window looking at the mountains surrounding the areas. They really were breathtaking with their sheer size.

Ten minutes later the bus pulled up to Yuko's stop and she exited. The breeze was calm against her skin as she walked to her home. When she walked in the door she called out "I'm home" and got no reply. Walking into the kitchen she saw a note on the counter.

"Yuko your father had to go to a meeting in Toronto today; got the call after you left for school, but he should be back in two days. I'm out at the local supermarket looking for some things to stock up our empty pantry. I should be home before six. Love you sweetie, mom.

After reading the note Yuko laughed. Their pantry was empty; all they managed to grab was some food for several days after they left the airport the previous day. She had expected her mother to do the shopping during the day after she left for school.

Grabbing her bag Yuko headed upstairs to her room. Tossing it on the floor she sat down at her desk and began sorting through the CDs which lay on the surface. Once those were organized, she turned to the small pile of papers. Most of which weren't of any use to her, so she put them off to the side for disposal. The door opened downstairs, so Yuko headed out and saw her mother walking in.

"Oh, hi sweetie" she said with a groan. "Perfect timing, I need help with these groceries."

"Sure, no problem" Yuko replied with a small smile.

Thankfully, her father had been able to purchase a small car off a local who was upgrading to the newer version of the same thing for the current year. It was convenient having a car for transportation. Grabbing some bags from the trunk Yuko walked back into the house where she saw her mother sitting in the living room chair, looking very tired.

"Are you alright?' Yuko asked, setting the bags on the kitchen table.

"Yes, I'm fine; I've just been really busy over the last few hours so I'm very tired."

Yuko went back to the car to grab the last bag of food. When she returned, she saw her mother taking some of the food to the pantry. Some of it was canned and prepared foods, mainly soup and bread. Yuko grabbed some bags of meat and placed them in the freezer under the fridge. They finished unloading everything in about twenty minutes. After they finished Yuko's mother went back to the couch and lay down, she did look very tired.

Yuko looked at the clock and saw that it was only half past four; they had lots of time before dinner. The sun had come out, so Yuko decided to go take a walk outside. Leaving a note on the table, as her mother had fallen asleep; Yuko grabbed her coat off the hook in the hall and started down the street. She wasn't worried; she often went for walks down the valley areas in Japan so she knew her mother wouldn't mind.

Strolling down the street she came across a large field where some kids were playing soccer. They were all in t-shirts and shorts.

They obviously don't mind this cool breeze. Yuko thought as the wind picked up slightly; sending a cold chill down her spine and forcing her to zip up the rest of her jacket. She saw the kids run over to some bags and pull out some long sleeve shirts as well as some longer, but still loose, pants. Yuko smiled at her quick assumption that they weren't affected by the wind. Continuing down the street Yuko looked up at the mountains off to her left. White clouds hid their peaks from view and made them appear even mightier. She saw several paths leading down the forests she passed on her walk; she decided to venture down some of them sometime. Coming up to a larger set of trees she saw a sign posted by a wider path than the previous ones. "Long Pine Forest; nature's wonders await you within."

"A tourist calling card" Yuko said to herself with a smirk. The trees were very large however, get far enough into the forest and you may end up walking at night. A cool breeze came through the trees and whisked the pines with them directly at Yuko's face. The smell that penetrated her was fresh. As she stood there admiring the pine scent she saw a deer appear from the labyrinth of trees in front of her sniffing the ground. Looking up with two black eyes it locked its gaze upon her for a few seconds. Having her camera in her pocket Yuko decided to take a picture of the creature while she had the opportunity. Rare shots like this never came around often. The deer stared at her with curiosity; it didn't seem scared of the camera as Yuko took it out of her pocket and pointed it at its face. After the shutter clasped down the deer fled into the trees at the sound of the crack. Looking up after another cold breeze struck her spine, making her shiver; she saw some clouds rolling in overhead. Not wanting to get caught in a storm Yuko headed home.

Yuko's mother was still asleep on the couch when she walked in the front door, checking the clock Yuko saw that she had only been gone for about half an hour.

It's odd how time seems to go by so fast sometimes she thought as she headed upstairs. Lying down on her bed Yuko began to think about the day and what had occurred. She liked the school she was in and knew that she'd get used to the teachers. The Kyoto International School she had attended back in Japan was a school she missed. The activities were fun, and all her friends were back there, probably having a good time playing for their school teams "The Dragons." It was a small school and so was the one here, which was a good thing. Yuko knew she could quickly meet everyone and possibly even make new friends.

Should be easier for me to get along with everyone as we all are in the same stage of our lives.

Then a new thought struck her, *Why did Max* seem so

MICHAEL MCGEE

bothered by something today?

She decided she would ask Max about that tomorrow.

Chapter Three

THE BUS CAME on time the next morning. The sun shone on the mountains making their snowy peaks shine. A light breeze kept things cool. It was a perfect day. The bus drove up to Max's house where she was waiting outside. She wore some slightly darker clothing than the previous day while Yuko was wearing slightly lighter clothing.

"Trying to stand out today?" Max asked as she took a seat next to Yuko.

"Not really" Yuko replied "Just trying to fit in."

Max didn't respond insisting on keeping her gaze out the window.

"Hey, can I ask you something?" Yuko said, turning to

Max as the bus began accelerating down the road.

"What?" she replied, barely turning to face her.

"You looked really bothered yesterday by something; I'm sorry about being pushy, but why was that?"

"I told you not to get involved in that."

"I know it's just; I'm curious."

"Please just don't pursue it anymore, trust me, it's better that way."

The bus pulled up to the school, Max jumped up and ran off without another word. The Sisters were waiting outside the main doors trying to look tough. Yuko and Max tried to pass by them, but they were stopped by an arm to the chest.

"What is it now Victoria?" Max asked, turning to face the one who stuck her arm out in front of them.

"What were you two talking about on the bus, you trying to get this nobody on your good side?" She asked with her two partners glaring down behind her.

"We were having a conversation, that's all you need to know." Max replied staring back at Victoria.

"Well, I sure hope you weren't talking about what you did when you were younger," Mandy replied from above Victoria.

Max remained silent, she didn't move, just stared.

"Come on Max lets go." Yuko tried tugging on her arm, but it was no good, she was frozen. "Max?"

"Well look at that, I guess the past does follow you wherever you go" laughed Mandy as the three of them headed inside.

ANGEL OF DARKNESS

"Max you alright?" Yuko asked, shaking Max's arm trying to get her attention or just some reaction from her. Max jumped a second later startling her. "Max?"

She turned her head to look at Yuko, her face was in shock.

"I'm fine." She said, shaking her head. "Just a bad memory."

"Are you sure? You look really stunned."

"I'll be fine, come on we don't want to be late for math." With that she began heading off into the school, Yuko close behind.

The day went by smoothly after that. The Sisters stayed out of their way which made both girls feel a little more at ease. Mathematics class began with some long division and multiplication, Yuko did not enjoy that.

"Lengthy problems are my weakness" she muttered in frustration. Construction class was more engaging than that of the previous day. The students watched some films on simple safety guidelines on some of the power tools and machines they would be using in the shop later in the term. Mr. Johnson then assigned everyone a machine as a project where they would have to each present, in their own words, additional guidelines and information on their respective machine. Yuko chose the table saw as she was interested in that the most, Max picked what was called the miter saw.

Once the bell rang for lunch the class hurried out to the core of the school. Yuko held a table that Max picked out for them, far away from The Sisters, while Max went to get lunch from the cafeteria again. Some girls came by and asked to join the table as Yuko took out her lunch. "That would be great," she replied, to which the two girls sat down.

"You're new here aren't you?" asked a tall blonde haired girl. "I'm asking because I've never seen you around here before."

"Megan you're supposed to introduce yourself before you ask something like that." The other girl with brown hair said.

"Right sorry, I'm Megan it's nice to meet you." Megan said with a guilty look.

"I'm Ashley," followed the other girl turning to Yuko.

"Nice to meet you. My name is Yuko and to answer your question Megan; yes I am new here just arrived here to Canada a few days ago."

"Awesome we've both lived here our whole lives. Where are you from?" Ashley asked quickly.

"Kyoto, Japan"

"Kyoto, wow that's a pretty big city isn't it?"

"Ya, it's pretty large compared to this place." Yuko replied.

"Come on Megan you know that Kyoto is one of the largest cities in the world."

"I know, I wanted to sound surprised that's all" Megan replied with another guilty look.

"Well, welcome to Alberta, Canada." Ashley said.

Max had returned and suddenly Megan and Ashley looked worried.

"Hey Max," Yuko said, turning to her "Do you know

ANGEL OF DARKNESS

Megan and Ashley?" She pointed to the two girls sitting next to her when she noticed their faces were enveloped by dread. "Are you guys alright?"

Megan and Ashley turned as Max looked at them with a quick attempt at a smile before sitting down; the girls calmed down slightly.

"We're fine," Megan said.

"Yes, I know them, they're in my forensic science class" Max replied as she put her chicken wraps from the cafeteria down.

"What is that class about?" Yuko asked.

"It's investigation stuff, police work" Ashley replied, still looking fearful of Max. "We learn about blood splatter patterns, insects and their relation to dead bodies, different ways on how investigators can find clues that are invisible to the naked eye. It's all very interesting stuff and Max here is at the top of our class."

"Really?" Yuko asked, turning back to Max.

"I find it very interesting so I to do well in it."

"I always thought you joined that class because of what happened…" Megan began to say before Ashley elbowed her in the ribs.

"You know she doesn't want to talk about that." Ashley spat out at her. Max got up and began walking away.

"Wait, I'm sorry I didn't mean to." Megan cried. Max continued to walk away, her head down.

"What happened when she was younger?" Yuko asked. "The Sisters were bullying her about the same topic this morning and she looked like she was ready to scream."

Ashley and Megan looked at each other before turning back.

"I think that's something you should ask her yourself." Ashley said, looking upset with herself.

"She takes what happened very personally and when the rumors began to spread everyone here began to see her differently and have been afraid of her ever since. We even get slight chills when she's near and we can't help it." Megan followed.

"Why?" Yuko asked.

"We should be getting off the bells about to ring and we need to grab our books." Ashley said quickly.

"It was nice meeting you Yuko" Megan followed as she got up with Ashley.

"Thanks, it was nice to meet you too," Yuko replied with a small smile but still wondering about what they had said about Max. As she finished her lunch, she began walking to her locker to grab her books for social studies. She didn't see Max, their lockers were beside each other.

She must already be in the room. Not knowing where to go Yuko asked one of the passing students who pointed her in the right direction. Max wasn't in the room when Yuko arrived. After class Yuko had gym. She saw Max walk into the dressing room ahead of her. "Hey Max."

"Hey" she replied, not turning to her.

"I thought we had social class together, but you weren't there."

Max didn't reply, she just stared into her locker, as if searching for something.

ANGEL OF DARKNESS

"Listen I'd like to have time to myself for this class if you don't mind; I just need time to think."

"Sure" Yuko said quietly "If that's what you want."

The class went smoothly; the teacher simply went over a course outline that explained what they would be covering over the next few months. It mainly consisted of simple sports, but the teacher was constantly stating that their skills weren't going to get them as many grade scores as their participation, he couldn't stop saying that.

"Pretty clear that he wants us all to give everything a chance at least and not wimp out" Yuko overheard one of the students whisper to another student.

The class ended with an introduction to their first activity, ball hockey. Hockey was apparently the sport of the country and most of the students were excited for it. Yuko however had never skated in her life. Thankfully, this version of the game was indoors and wouldn't require ice skates. That would be for a later time when the rinks opened in the winter.

After the class went back to the change rooms, Yuko decided to try and cheer Max up. "Hey Max, I was wondering if you'd be able to show me around the town?"

"Why do you want me to do that?" Max asked, turning to her.

"Well, I don't know my way around here as I just moved here, and you said you've lived here a long time, so I thought you'd know your way around. Plus, you seem to have been having a bad day these last few hours so I thought it might cheer you up to do something."

Max stood there for a second before replying "can we do

that tomorrow? We get out of school early on Fridays so we can have more time then."

"Tomorrow works." Yuko replied.

"Thanks," she grabbed her bag and went outside leaving Yuko standing still in her gym clothes.

The next day went by very quickly. When Yuko and Max walked out of school the sun was still high in the sky. Max led the way past the bus and down a road that led to the center of the town. Most of the students from the school headed down the same route; Yuko thought she might see Megan and Ashley again.

"This area is where the shopping district begins." Max told Yuko as they walked down the street. "It's where most of the clothing and furniture shops are."

Staring into the store windows Yuko saw a variety of winter clothing from heavy jackets to slimmer sweaters and even some blankets for when it got chilly out. All of them had some sort of wildlife aspect to them whether it was the forests, mountains, lakes, valleys, or wildlife. She mentioned this to Max.

"The people of this town value nature and they take pride in preserving both it and the animals that inhabit it."

"There are a lot of wolves on those shirts; do wolves live around here?"

"They inhabit the mountain areas around her. Sometimes they wander down into our backyards. They never come too close though as they are often careful around humans, unless they're hunting that is." Yuko slightly shivered at that last bit.

As they continued down the street, they reached some

ANGEL OF DARKNESS

restaurants and candy shops. Max wasn't really interested; but Yuko checked out the menus that some of the restaurants had placed outside their entrance. Yuko wanted to check out this one place called White Peak, but Max cut her off saying it was expensive and they couldn't afford restaurant food.

The girls decided to stop by a small burger joint where it wasn't as expensive. According to Max it would have cost them over forty dollars at least for just the two of them if they stopped at White Peak. Yuko didn't mind, she was just happy that Max seemed to be in a good mood and not down about what everyone was saying about her earlier.

The sun was getting low, so Max decided to head home. Yuko walked partway with her; trying to avoid the urge to clarify what was bothering her about the secret Max was keeping from her.

Chapter Four

THE SUN ROSE early as Zeus walked out into the clouds. The third day had come, and it was time to meet with the Gods of the North to hear what they had to say. As Zeus walked towards the gate of Olympus he paused and waited. A few minutes' later two circles appeared on either side of him, one sapphire blue the other one amethyst black. Poseidon spun out of the sapphire one with his trident in hand while Hades faded from the amethyst, his body forming from the mist. Zeus looked to his brothers, and they nodded in turn. Zeus held up the blue crystal given to him by Hugin. As the sun's rays touched the gem the three Gods were pulled into its sudden gravitational field and were sucked away in a flurry of light. All three Gods were pulled faster than the speed of light towards the sky, the sky turned to darkness, the darkness to galaxy. When the Gods saw their destination, they flipped in unison as they crashed their feet upon a rainbow bridge. As the three gazed at the golden city before them they saw someone approach.

"And I half expected you to be late oh great Gods of Earth" said the golden armored figure whose eyes gleamed with light.

"Heimdall you bright old geezer you," replied Zeus with a smile as he took the guardian of Asgard into his arms.

Heimdall laughed as he turned to Hades and Poseidon in turn each of whom he shared an equal form of welcome.

"Please come this way the others are waiting" Heimdall said after receiving a crushing greeting from the sea God.

"So, what is this meeting about?" spoke Hades as he glided along the bridge with his brothers alongside their escort.

"I was not told; Odin rarely gives out information regarding such meetings these days; he simply asked me to escort you to the grand hall where the meeting will take place."

"So, you're still an errand boy for that old man?" Poseidon asked as he washed over the city streets.

"I am the great guardian of Asgard, and my loyalty is to my king, his word is my command." Heimdall replied as his voice grew deep.

"I apologize I simply meant that you still follow your leader's word with extreme loyalty."

ANGEL OF DARKNESS

"Yes, it is an honor to serve under the watcher of the nine realms."

"An honor that must not be taken lightly." Zeus spoke.

"Indeed" Heimdall replied in turn as the four walked through the main palace doors.

Heimdall led the three Gods through several passageways and corridors till finally they reached a door with a golden eagle carved into its frame. Heimdall pushed the doors open to reveal a circular room where a round table lay in the center with chairs equally spread around it. Light shone through several large windows around the room and there sitting in the seat opposite the door sat Odin with his wife Freya, and his sons Loki and Thor at his side. To the left of the entrance stood Ra, Sobek, and Anubis the Egyptian Gods of Earth. To the right stood Athena, Goddess of wisdom; Chronos, keeper of time; and Mercury, messenger of the Roman Gods.

"Thank you Heimdall, let no one enter this room" Odin said in a calm but strong voice. Heimdall bowed and exited the room closing the doors behind him.

"You three made it just in time" Odin said, addressing the Greek Gods who all turned to face him.

"Why are these ones here?" asked Hades pointing to the Egyptian, Roman, and fellow Greek Gods.

"I have asked them to attend as they may be able to provide some insight as to what we've gathered here to address." Odin pointed to Athena and the Egyptians. "Chronos wishes to keep record of what is said here in the Vault of Time. Mercury is here to spread the word to all other Gods; if what we discuss here today becomes evident that we need to be mindful of it."

"Just what is that?" Zeus asked not turning his gaze from Odin.

"Please sit and we will begin." Odin said pointing around the table; all the Gods sat, and silence fell around them.

"As we all know it has been many years since there was a gathering such as this." Odin spoke, breaking the silence.

"I would hardly call this a gathering" spoke Anubis in a foul voice. "A gathering usually consists of more than merely thirteen individuals."

"True, but we all were present when you three were shown what you assumed was the future of us all" spoke Thor pointing towards the Greeks.

"The future of all of us?" asked Poseidon "What do you mean by that?"

"Have you forgotten fish man about what you were shown within that secret basin you hold behind your strongest laid traps?" spoke Chronos.

"That is what you have called us here to address?" Zeus spoke turning to Odin, as his brother clenched his fist at the timekeeper's words.

"Yes, I have called you here to discuss just that." Odin replied, his face still calm which puzzled Zeus.

"It has been far too long, and nothing has occurred since you spoke of that event." Loki called out.

"I don't see you not having a possible part in that." Hades spoke deeply pointing at the trickster God. "If I remember you caused great disruption to the peace your

ANGEL OF DARKNESS

adopted father over there worked hard to achieve."

"He may not be my father by birth!" retaliated Loki "but I have accepted him as my father and her as my mother." He pointed towards Freya.

"That's enough!!" bellowed Odin before the two villains began clashing. Both Loki and Hades sat back down. "Now will you hear us out?"

Zeus looked towards Hades who sighed and nodded. "Proceed."

"As we all know, you three were shown a vision of a great being attacking you and your domains." The Gods remained silent. "Yet it has been over two thousand years, and nothing has occurred that even hints towards the rise of such an enemy."

"It may have been a long time but that doesn't mean it won't still occur." Poseidon replied.

"Zeus, you were shown a bright sky that was covered in shadows correct?" Sobek asked, turning towards him.

"Yes, I was."

"Yet the sun of the Earth has not become blanketed by darkness except on those rare occasions where the moon overlaps against the sun. I believe humans call this a solar eclipse; and even then there has been no disturbance in the balance of nature." Spoke Ra with a birdlike shriek in his voice.

"That is true," spoke Zeus as he rested his chin on his fist.

"Sea God you were shown a vast body of water being enveloped by a torrent of flame." Spoke Mercury with a flurry of wind in his voice.

"That I was, and I know what you want to say, and yes the waters of the world still flow with no resistance." Spoke Poseidon as he turned to face Mercury.

"Finally, Hades" spoke Freya in a soft voice. "You were shown a figure cloaked in shadows cross into your land and cut you with a white blade which severed your soul from your body?"

"Yes." Spoke Hades in a grim voice. "You have all repeated what we shared with you all those years ago, a good reminder I thank you for that, but this still does not explain why we are here now."

"We have gathered here to drop this matter altogether." Thor spoke as he twirled his hammer, Mjolnir, in his hands.

The Greeks turned towards Thor with open mouths. "Drop the matter?" they spoke in unison.

"Yes" Odin spoke "We believe what you were shown was nothing more than a falsehood."

"A falsehood?" spoke Poseidon in shock and rage "The Ancients have never been wrong in predicting anything before, why would they show us a future that is not to be?"

"What proof do you have that there is a being in pursuit of us all and the peace we have established through intense combat and war?" replied Thor.

Zeus, Hades, and Poseidon remained silent; what proof did they have?

"The items that my eternal judge holder, Ma At, holds upon her have not been swayed or drawn towards anything in over three millennia; that was before you were even

ANGEL OF DARKNESS

shown your vision." Spoke Anubis.

"Those items are the judgment of the good and evil in mortals, why would they sway in response to anything we have seen?" asked Hades, turning towards the jackal headed human.

"They have the power to detect extreme levels of darkness within the world," replied Anubis as he faced the empty eyes of the dead king. "They would have detected something if it had occurred, but they have not been swayed even the slightest.

"The Nile's waters and the rivers of the world have not been altered even the slightest" Spoke the Nile God Sobek. "Nor has the oceans been swept away by flame as you foresaw sea God."

"The seas and rivers of the world have not been altered, true, but that is still no reason to say these events still may not come to pass." Poseidon replied.

"While that is all true" Zeus spoke with a glance around the table. "What difference does it make that there has been little to no disturbance in the balance? Why should we ignore a possible threat that could bring about our very end?"

"The being that we were shown was powerful; that much was very clear" followed Hades.

"It may not be here at this moment but who's to say it will not come at all?" Poseidon spoke following his brother's lead.

The room fell silent. Loki spun his blades on his finger, Chronos glanced at the wheel of time on his hand, Ra stroked his feathers. Finally, after several minutes Athena spoke.

"There may well be a being of great power approaching; but until some sort of disturbance is detected there should be no cause for alarm."

"You are the Goddess of wisdom, wiser than all of us; even me," a shocked Zeus spoke. "Why do you not trust the wisdom of the Ancients when they have shown us a great evil?"

"Zeus, you have been endlessly training to combat a force that may never come for another hundred thousand years. You are pushing yourself out of fear and are not thinking logically."

"Odin you are constantly preparing yourself for the coming of Ragnarök, why does this being not frighten you? It could be the bringer of that very event" Hades asked the old man sitting across from him.

"I am constantly preparing myself for that moment, and when it comes there will be nothing to stop it; however, I do not prepare out of fear. I am constantly acknowledging that possibility; but I do not believe this shadow you saw is the bringer of it."

"Why do you not fear this being?" Hades said.

"Because no evidence of such a being has been presented at any point in our time since you spoke of it all those years ago." Odin exclaimed.

The room fell silent as all Gods wondered what to say next.

"What if there never is proof?" Zeus spoke softly under his breath but not softly enough as Poseidon heard it clearly.

ANGEL OF DARKNESS

"Brother, you know what we saw may come to be. But they are right. Without any clue as to what we saw even occurring; there is no point in worrying about what may never come to fruition for another thousand years."

Zeus pondered this idea for a moment before addressing Athena. "I cannot deny that you may be right. There may be a powerful being of our demise but until we learn more, we should be cautious and open to any changes in the worlds we currently oversee."

"Then do we have an agreement that we will not discuss this matter anymore and this being you saw in your vision is nothing more than a falsehood?" asked Odin with a smirk obviously having heard what Zeus said.

"A falsehood, but-" Zeus began to say before Hades cut him off.

"I believe for the time being we should agree it may be false as we do not have any knowledge as to what we even may face."

"So, all those in favor of calling this meeting over and we need not worry about this being of darkness?" Odin asked, glancing around the room. All hands were raised except for Zeus, Hades, and Poseidon. "Well, that is a majority vote. Dismissed."

Odin banged his staff on the ground and took Freya's hand before exiting the room. Athena bowed to Zeus before being swallowed by a river of light to return to Olympus. Chronos clicked the wheels on his staff to store the meeting temporarily until he could return to his headquarters to deposit it into long term storage of time. Anubis opened a hole to the Egyptian afterlife beneath him and fell through it, returning to his placement of judgment. Loki disappeared in a puff of smoke, Ra a pillar of light, Sobek a river conjured from below his feet, and Thor flying out the window by his hammer's handle.

"Odin, why did we have to come here by teleportation crystal? Surely we could have used our own methods to come to this place?" Hades questioned Odin before he could leave through the door behind them.

"I've strengthened my defenses around Asgard to prevent attacks from unwanted guests. The crystal I gave you is one of the only items that can bypass the barrier and allow people within the city. I just lowered the barrier temporarily so you may leave in your own method." Odin spoke towards the king of the dead as he exited the hall.

"We should return to our domains now." Hades spoke; rising from his seat.

"That sounds like a very good idea" replied Poseidon. "Let's get out of this place of embarrassment and deception."

Zeus remained seated at the table while his brothers parted behind him in a flurry of darkness and watery portals. "Why did these fools think that this evil is not approaching? The proof may not be here at this very moment, but the Ancients have never been wrong before. Why would they show us something if it wasn't meant to be?" Zeus thought this through carefully as the sun began sinking over the golden city, replacing the light with darkness.

Chapter Five

"ARE YOU EATING it or playing with it? Her mother asked at breakfast the next morning looking at her over the paper.

"Sorry just thinking." Yuko replied, grabbing a spoonful of her cereal.

"About what?"

"Just something two students said about my new friend who I met the other day at school."

"Is it that Max girl you told us about?" asked her father as he put his coffee down. He had returned home from his business trip the previous night. The order they had placed came on time without delay. That made the bosses in Japan happy it also meant that they would not be behind on next year's model. It would apparently be a new Toyota.

"Yes, it is" replied Yuko looking up at her father. "Some things about her that I find hard to believe."

"What sort of things?"

"She has a past that makes everyone around her frightened and afraid. I don't know why and I'm worried that Max will be angry with me if I ask her."

"Maybe it would be a good idea to ask her then and see what happens." Her mother replied with the caring voice she always used when she was trying to be comforting. "There is nothing wrong with asking."

"I know there's just something about that thought it doesn't seem to feel right. I don't know why." Yuko replied.

Both her parents looked at each other; they both seemed confused as to what was causing Yuko's own confusion.

"If it doesn't feel right then it probably isn't" her father told her. Yuko looked up at the calm face he put on. "Sometimes things just aren't meant to be discovered and are best left to those who do know what the problem is. This seems like it is personal for your friend and if it feels wrong to ask about it because of that you should not worry so much about it."

Yuko thought about that for a moment, was she just being too concerned about her friend's problems?

"You're right," she said after a minute. "Maybe this is something I shouldn't be worried about. Thanks Dad."

"You can always ask me for help with anything you need." He replied with a smile which Yuko mirrored.

It had rained overnight so the bus had to drive slower

ANGEL OF DARKNESS

than usual. Yuko didn't mind as she glanced at Max who sat ahead of her. She tried to enjoy the Max she knew now rather than the one everyone else seemed to be afraid of.

The Sisters weren't outside of the school that day which was nice. Max certainly seemed more at ease during their math class without those three irritating her first thing in the morning. During Industrial Arts, the class moved out of the shop into the computer lab where they did research on their assigned machines from the previous days. Both Yuko and Max enjoyed it as that meant they were one step closer to the fun stuff. The rest of the day went smoothly, but that all changed when Max's phone rang when they exited the school at the end of the day.

"Hello" she said into the receiver as she and Yuko stood off to the side of the other students leaving for the day. "Is everything alright?"

Yuko looked up as a strange feeling of worry shot through her.

After a minute of silence Max's face turned to shock.

"I'll be home as fast as I can." With that she hung up dashed towards the bus.

"What happened?"

Max didn't reply; she just kept running with Yuko in pursuit. Max dashed inside the bus, knocking several students out of the way, and grabbed the closest seat to the door. She remained quiet for the ride and didn't acknowledge Yuko asking what had happened beside her. As soon as the bus came to a stop at her house Max dashed off and inside without a glance back to Yuko, which just made Yuko wonder more about what the emergency was.

MICHAEL MCGEE

Max didn't show up to school the next day. Yuko just became more concerned about her; all thoughts about not wanting to interfere with Max's life were just shot down by her general habit of wanting to be a helpful person. Back in Japan she had always helped those who appeared to need help whether that was lifting heavy objects or talking to someone, usually close to her, that had had a bad day or was really stressed about something. Max seemed to be having one of those days except this seemed more extreme than ever. Something was wrong, and Yuko generally wanted to be of assistance to her in overcoming that problem. Just as she began to get her mind together about how to try and help her friend, she remembered her father's words from the previous day.

"Sometimes things aren't meant to be discovered and are best left to those who do know what the problem is."

That was what he had said. He was right; she was being too overly concerned about this when it wasn't her place to be involved. Whatever the problem was she was certain that Max would be able to handle it. She headed to her science class which was on the lower level of the school in the corner of the building. The class lulled onward as the teacher, Mr. West, talked to the class about biology and the study of different species in the world and their numerous categories within the animal kingdom. Being tired from worrying about Max all night didn't help Yuko concentrate at all and the teacher's voice only made her drowsier. As the teacher moved on to the subject of some of the native animals such as the mountain goats and red fox, Yuko's eyes slowly drifted shut.

She woke up standing in a forest. Snow covered the earth and trees around her. Yuko couldn't figure out where she was or how she got there; last thing she remembered was being in a biology class and the teacher was lecturing the class about red foxes. Their fur being dense and fluffy to the touch; but that did not excuse their nature of being powerful predators to prey such as deer mice. Yuko turned as the sound of snow being crunched rang through her ears. She saw a small pack of red foxes behind her; darting through the trees with their bodies whisking the snowy field around them.

"This must be a dream, if it is, then how do I get out of it?"

Yuko tried to force herself awake by closing and opening her eyes; but was unable to wake up. Turning back to the foxes she decided to follow them from afar. Maybe they knew, somehow, how to wake her up. As she followed them, the foxes suddenly turned to her, their black eyes gazed upon her. Neither party made a move. They just stared at each other. Then their red fur straightened up on their backs. Teeth barred as they growled towards her the fox's bodies erupted into flame. Their backs illuminated by the light of the yellow and orange that shot from their hides. Beautiful and deadly all at the same time. Out of fear Yuko began to run. She heard the foxes dashing after her with superior speed, foxes main hunting method was based on movement so running was not a good idea, but what choice did she have. Yuko continued to dash through the trees as the foxes gained on her.

"Yuko!!" she heard the leader of the pack yell behind her; this dream became a nightmare. Losing her footing, Yuko's body hit the ground. Turning around she heard the fox scream her name as its open jaw struck at her neck, teeth sharper than steel.

MICHAEL MCGEE

"YUKO!!!"

Her eyes burst open. She was on the floor, her legs scrunched up into a ball, people all around her staring at her. Mr. West was next to her with his hand on her shoulder.

"Are you alright?" He asked with a calm voice.

"Yeah, sorry just fell asleep, had a late night."

"Had a nightmare?"

"Yes. It's nothing though."

"What kind of nightmare?" A male student asked looking down at her "You were curled up into a ball and screaming pretty rapidly."

"It's nothing, I'm fine. Sorry for worrying all of you."

"Maybe you should go see the nurse." Mr. West suggested placing his hand on her forehead. "Your head feels rather warm."

She did feel a bit dizzy after all that, and sweaty. "That might be a good idea."

"Mike can you take her there?" Mr. West asked the student who had explained to Yuko what she was doing on the ground.

"Sure thing, here do you need a hand?" Mike asked, holding out his hand to Yuko which she took as he pulled her to her feet. Mike walked with her down the hallway towards the first aid room where a middle-aged woman was working on organizing a set of first aid supplies. "Hey Mrs. Hinley; can you help us?"

"Sure, what's the problem?"

ANGEL OF DARKNESS

"Yuko here is having a headache at the moment; we were wondering if you had some ice to possibly help her."

"I do have some ice packs, take a seat here," Mrs. Hinley pulled a chair out from underneath a table and turned it around so Yuko could easily take a seat.

"Thanks Mike." Yuko said to him as she sat up.

"No problem."

Mrs. Hinley came back and handed Yuko a small cold pack which she put on her head. Mike walked out of the room to let them have some privacy. "Are you feeling sick at all?" Mrs. Hinley asked as she took a seat.

"No, I just..."

"What is it?"

"It's embarrassing; never mind."

"Nothing is embarrassing, what happened?"

"I fell asleep in class and had a nightmare; only it wasn't like what you'd normally think about when I say that."

"Why is that?"

"It felt like it was real. I've had similar dreams like this before and they all have a similar feeling when I wake up. Only the dreams seem to keep building up on each other."

"Building up, what do you mean?"

"The first time I was just in a forest, and something jumped at me, I didn't see what it was. The next one the forest was darker and the only thing I saw was teeth. After that I saw something dashing through the trees as I ran. This time I saw foxes which burst into flames before calling my name and then jumping at me with their teeth. It sounds odd but it seems like something might be trying to tell me something in a strange way." Yuko remained silent after that, she felt like an idiot.

I mean who would believe anything so absurd?

"So, this dream has been piecing itself together in fragments and each time you've gotten a clearer vision of what it is showing you?" Mrs. Hinley asked, looking directly at Yuko.

"Yes, I know it sounds like something only a kid would worry about."

"You also said it felt real, how did it feel?"

"It only felt real one time and that was a while ago. I just woke up with my legs stiff, like someone glued them down and put a splint onto them."

"That is odd, is it possible you just moved a lot in reaction to what you were seeing."

"That's what I thought as well, but I still don't understand why it seems like it's as if something is putting together a puzzle in my mind. And I'm supposed to understand it."

They both remained silent for a while. The ice pack had lost its chill, so Yuko put it down on the table next to her. Her headache was gone which made her feel a bit better, but it couldn't fix the confusion that was still settling into her.

After a while Mrs. Hinley looked at Yuko and said "I don't really know if this is an answer, but maybe this is something that you can't rid yourself of. It might be something you can't fight, what usually gets you thinking about this forest?"

ANGEL OF DARKNESS

Yuko stared at her for a moment. "I guess it might be the stress and fear of having to move here from my home country."

"Where was that if I may ask?"

"Japan."

"You and your family moved here recently?"

"Yes, we arrived a little over a week ago."

"And have you thought about forests in the past?"

"Not really, this town is surrounded by forestry, so I guess that is what got me thinking about it. Just when I see the nature around here, I can't help but admire and think about it."

"Is it possible that this new surrounding that is constantly around us may be altering your thoughts slightly? I've never been to Japan myself, but I can imagine it is a different scenery that surrounds you there."

"Maybe, I've always read that the mountains and forestry was amazing over here in this country and when I actually saw it I was completely entranced by its view."

"That sounds like the reason as to why you are thinking about a forest and because this is a new country to you it's natural to be frightened about it."

"What about the foxes that are appearing in the nightmares, what do you think those are representing?"

"Probably an image that is being created by your fear. Are you afraid of foxes?"

"No, I'm not"

"Must be something that represents your fear of the

forests and condenses it into something to be feared."

"What can help me with this fear?"

"Go out and explore. See the forests, the rivers, the lakes; become familiar with the land you now call your home. If you feel scared it is because you have yet to become accustomed to this new area. If you take time and see it for how you see it through your eyes that will clear out the fear of the unknown."

Yuko thought about that for a minute. It was true that she feared what she still had not seen. "That does sound like it would work. Maybe I can ask the other students around here to show me around. My new friend Max already showed me some of the areas around here but maybe there are others who can show me."

"Sounds like you have a plan to get rid of this fear you have."

"Thanks, I feel better now that I've talked about it."

"My door is always open if you ever need help with anything."

Yuko smiled. With a bow she headed out of the room just in time to see Megan and Ashley heading over to a table for lunch.

Chapter Six

MAX RETURNED TO school the next day. She didn't look well as she walked into construction class where Yuko was handing in her report on the table saw to Mr. Johnson. She felt confident in her analysis of the table saw and all its components. She had included a section on the safety practices when using the machine; but decided she would leave that to the teacher if they were asked to present their reports on each machine. Max handed in her own report before walking over to her seat beside Yuko. She looked a bit more relaxed than she did the previous day.

"Are you alright?" Yuko asked her quietly.

"Yes, I'm fine. Sorry about the other day I just had something important to take care of. Family matters that haven't been fixed in a long time and can come up unexpectedly at any moment. I live with my father you see and he's not very well at the moment."

"What's wrong with him?"

"It's just…" she began before turning away. "No, never mind I don't want you to get involved in what my life is throwing at me these days."

"Are you sure there isn't anything I can do to help?"

"I'm sure; it's my business and no one else's."

"Ok, I'm sorry if I came off as being too concerning; my father says that is one of my greatest strengths but also one of my greatest weaknesses at the same time."

"My father says the opposite about me. That I'm not all that sympathetic most of the time and just look out for myself."

"That's funny." Yuko said. "Anyway, how did you think you did on your report for the machine you were assigned?"

"I think I did alright; I got an easy machine. What did you get again?"

"I got the table saw. What about you?"

"Miter saw." She pointed towards the machine as she said its name. A circular blade that was secured over top a table with extending arms on either side. "In my opinion it's one of the riskier machines we will have to use in this class."

"Why?" Yuko asked after looking at the guard over the blade which appeared to make it fairly safe to use.

"It's the way that the wood is placed along the table where the saw comes down when cutting. You have to hold it tight against the backboard otherwise it can snap the wood in half when you lower the blade. Apparently if that happens it can be very hazardous to the one using the machine."

"That sounds dangerous. The table saw also has its fair share of risks as well."

"I used that machine in junior high, as well as the miter saw, so I know that kickback can occur if the wood gets caught in the blade movement. If that happens you really have to be lucky that it doesn't deal major damage to your body."

"I read it can cause bruises and that's about the worst it gets."

"You read wrong then. Kickback sends a massive amount of force back at the saw's user; most people have lost use of their fingers to their entire hands for several weeks or longer. Other injuries can be internal and those can be hard to fix."

Yuko shivered as she heard that; the research she did explained some of those injuries but never in detail.

"You alright?" Max asked, noticing her shiver.

"Fine, just got a chill."

"From the table saw injuries?"

"Yes"

"Well don't worry too much about it. As long as you're careful when using the machine there shouldn't be any problems or wood headed your way."

"Yeah, I guess you're right."

The class went as Yuko expected; the teacher called up

students and asked them to present their machine research to the class. Because there were more students than machines there were duplicates in the presentations. The research each student did ended up varying slightly but for the most part it the same with each machine. Yuko and Max both presented their reports, and each received an approving nod from the teacher. Obviously, they had done a good job on their research. The class ended with five more students needing to present; they would do that the next day, however. Lunch time came around and when Max and Yuko took their seats they were quickly greeted by Ashley and Megan.

"Hey girls, mind if we join you?" Ashley asked with a slight look towards Max.

"Sure, that would be great" Yuko responded, also taking a slight glance in Max's direction while trying not to be obvious of her suspicion. Max looked up and the girls quickly turned their eyes away.

"You don't have to do that." She said, turning her eyes to the three of them. "You can join us if you'd like."

Ashley and Megan both took seats opposite the other two. Their shoulders tight, but they quickly relaxed as they sat down.

"So, how's your day going?" Megan asked the two across from her.

"It's going good." Max replied with a cold stare. "We just had construction class where we had to present a bunch of safety stuff related to the machines we're going to be using probably next week."

"That should be fun, what machines did you guys have

ANGEL OF DARKNESS

to research?"

"I had the miter saw." Max replied.

"Table saw." Yuko followed as Ashley and Megan turned to get her answer. "What class did you two just come from?"

"Science" Ashley told her. "We started getting into angles and their usage in reflections and refractions."

"That sounds more like math." Yuko replied as she took up some sushi from her lunch.

"It's physics, which is basically math with more complex formulas and a lot of conversions." Ashley explained. "You'll probably be getting into that pretty soon as well."

"I don't think for a while, we're still in biology talking about the different families that creatures of the world are categorized into." Yuko replied.

"Our teacher is rather slow on the course work." Max told them quickly. "But the notes he makes us take make things easier to understand."

"At least that makes it sound like a breeze for you two." Megan replied, taking a sip from her water bottle. "We have to try and make up our own notes based on what the teacher explains to us, which is a bit of a pain. But at least we can put it into our own words, which makes it easier."

The four of them talked about what they were going to do after school that day. Max had to go take care of business at home, Ashley had volleyball practice, Megan had to run errands for her family, and Yuko didn't have anything planned.

"Why don't you tag along with me for a while then?" Megan suggested.

"Sure, sounds good," Yuko replied as the bell rang for the next class to begin.

After school Megan and Yuko headed towards the shopping district of the town. Clouds had rolled in, so it was a bit colder than the morning had been.

"Hey Yuko" Megan said as they walked out of the convenience store with some groceries. "Can I ask you something?"

"What is it?"

"You said you came here from Japan right?"

"That's right."

"What was it like over there?"

"Busy, a lot busier than over here."

"You said you were from Kyoto right?"

"That's right."

"Nice, I heard that is one of the best tourist locations for people who travel to Japan. Is that true?"

"Yes it is. Mainly for the temples and gardens that are within the city."

"Which ones are your favorite?"

"I'd have to say the Nazen-Ji, it's a Zen garden."

"What's a Zen garden?"

"It's a rock garden."

"Rock garden? What kind of garden is that when you think of a garden you think of flowers."

"Well for us we see them as a real image of any kind of symbolism. We see them as a way towards the abstract composition of natural objects in a space. In simple terms it's a way to incite meditation upon those who enter the garden. We say that one achieves enlightenment when they see all fifteen stones within the garden at the same time."

"Your people are very spiritual, aren't they?"

"We see value in everything around us and always devote all that we have to whatever we pursue. What is it that you believe or follow in your life?"

"I follow the religion of Christianity. It's a simple religion that teaches us to see everyone as equal and to forgive acts of hatefulness and anger."

"That seems like it leads to a very peaceful world."

"It leads to a place of eternal peace where the end of all suffering awaits us. Only problem is that this world is tough and it's difficult to make that place real here on earth."

"Maybe it's not about what is ahead of you but more about what is before you. You need to see the world for what it is and don't lose track of what is in front of you."

"That sounds exactly like how it's supposed to be. See the world as it is and accept it for what it gives us."

"Seems like our religious beliefs are pretty similar."

"I guess so."

They both laughed as they continued down the road towards a burger joint to get an afterschool snack. As they walked out, they bumped into Victoria and her two friends.

"Sorry" Megan said as she stepped back.

"Why don't you watch where you're going?" Victoria said before she noticed Yuko. "Well, looks like you've finally done the smart thing and moved away from Max the troublemaker."

"I don't see her as a troublemaker," Yuko told her. "I see her as a friend, and she had some business to take care of today, so I decided to hang with Megan who is also a great friend."

"What she still hasn't told you?" Mandy asked, moving to the front of the pack.

"Who?"

"Maxine, she hasn't told you what she's done?"

"No, she hasn't, and I find it's better to respect her privacy if it's something that bothers her that much!"

"Fine, have it your way." Victoria said with a grin. "Just know that anyone who spends time with her will always be seen as a troublemaker. No matter where, or who, they are." With that the Sisters walked off while laughing, leaving Yuko shocked. Was what happened to Max really that bad?

"Yuko?" She heard someone call. "Hey, Yuko, are you alright?" Yuko turned and saw Megan shaking her.

"Yeah, I'm okay."

"Those girls are total jerks. You shouldn't listen to them."

"They enjoy causing trouble for everyone."

"That's because they think they're better than everyone. So, they always enjoy standing out and being the center of attention. It really annoys me. Anyway, we should probably get going, I still have to get home and finish some homework."

"Same here" Yuko said. As the two began heading back to the school to catch the bus, which was picking up the volleyball team from their practice, Yuko managed to forget what the Sisters had said; but something still ached at the back of her mind, something she couldn't ignore.

"Hey Megan," Yuko said as she and Megan boarded the bus.

"Yes Yuko"

"Do you know…?" She began before thinking to herself that it might be rude to ask. She shouldn't get involved in other people's business. Yet she couldn't stop herself because of who she was.

"What?" Megan asked, starting to look slightly more curious.

"Do you know what happened to Max when she was younger?"

Megan turned away and looked at her feet. "Yes, well actually, I only know anything thanks to the rumors which circulated the school."

"Was it something as bad as The Sisters made it sound?"

"I don't know for certain; the story has been said several times and it seems like no one really knows the entire truth. I don't even know the exact story myself. Like I said I just followed the rumors. Max is the only one who knows the truth."

"What happened?"

"Why do you want to know? I mean you just moved here, and it seems like you want to try and start trouble with some people."

"Start trouble? Why would I be someone who wants to do that?"

MICHAEL MCGEE

"People saw you with Max on the first day, after that, it seemed to just spread. Rumors surfaced concerning you and her."

"I don't know what you mean. Max was just there as someone to help show me around and help me out during the first few days of school."

"Well, some people, not me that is, saw you with the person who everyone else feared. For some reason which I never understood myself; they all got scared of you as well."

"They got scared of me because I was around Max who everyone was already afraid of? What happened to Max? Tell me please."

"I can't because I don't know the truth. I don't know what really happened that day to her. If you want to know so badly why not try asking her yourself? She doesn't want to talk about it to anyone but maybe she'll talk to you."

"If she won't tell anyone why would tell me?"

"Because I think she might be able to open herself up to you."

"What makes you say that?"

"You seem to have a caring side that doesn't match that of others for some reason." Megan said as her face turned away to look outside. "I think Max seems to see that somehow and is slowly beginning to change. I mean she finally talked with us today for a short time at lunch."

"And you think that was her changing her ways?"

"You don't know her all that well, she doesn't know you, maybe she sees you as an escape from the glares she receives all the time." Megan said as she got up; the bus had arrived at her house. "See you tomorrow."

Yuko stared out the window for the remainder of the ride. Wondering if she really could help Max.

Yuko exited the bus earlier than usual, she decided to take a longer walk home. The wind picked up and swept through the area, Yuko felt something strange stir within her as the wind whipped her hair over her eyes. Almost like the wind was telling her to keep trying. Continue to try and find the truth. She glanced towards the peaks of the mountains, almost as if they were the milestone she had to cross, as the feeling within her faded away.

Chapter Seven

ZEUS PACED THE grand chambers of Olympus, thinking about what to do, what Odin had said.

"What proof do you have?"

The Ancients had predicted the rise of several events, and all came to pass. They had predicted two great wars which would thrust the world into total chaos would ensue. They predicted man would create weapons of great destruction; and the world placed on the very real edge of total annihilation. These events were predicted before he and his brothers were shown the vision of shadows darkening the realms; and yet they all came true beforehand and no such shadowy being had yet shown itself.

MICHAEL MCGEE

Zeus and his brothers didn't have proof the wars would ravage the earth. But what they did have were clues that revealed themselves in time.

"That's it" Zeus said out loud to himself. "We just need to stay open for any clues that may arise no matter how small those may be." Zeus sat down on his throne as he smirked for a second before a second thought struck him. "But what would those be?"

This was a prophecy that would be exceedingly difficult to foresee. The First World War had been drawn by political dispute by several powers of the mortal's realm. With the tensions Ares had felt between them he was positive a war would rage between them. Rage, they did just as it was foretold. The Second World War proceeded shortly after the first when single man took the German lose and made it personal. As a result, this one man rose up and became the leader of one of the evilest organizations to ever rise in the current millennia. Both the rise and destruction were felt by all the Olympians before it even began. Athena foresaw that the mortals of Earth would face great chaos.

Weapons of power did rise as foretold by the Ancients; what was not foretold was the devastation it placed on both the mortal and Godly realms. Even Hades was fearful of what would occur if they did nothing to stop it. Hundreds of man-made weapons detonating at once would drive the race of man to the end of life in an instant. At first the God of the dead was excited for this event; but soon realized that no matter how much he longed for mortal's death he still needed their belief and their fear of him so he could even exist.

All these events were preceded by great tension in the mortal world. But what clues would there be to detect darkness approaching. Eclipses, Sudden weather changes? It could be anything. But there had be something.

"I will not be seen as a fool in front of that old man!" Roared Zeus in anger and frustration.

"You won't have to," A voice said calmly.

Zeus turned his head to see Athena walking into the hall. "Wow, what happened here?"

Zeus looked around him; the entire hall was scorched with burn marks. "I um…." He began.

"Lost control of your own lightning in your frustrated state?"

"Yeah I did."

Athena burst out in a fist of laughter for a moment, the scene of her own father losing control like that after all these years was too great to pass over.

"What is so funny?"

"You" Athena said as she gained her breath back. "It's been a while since you last let your frustration control your own lightning."

Zeus thought about it for a second; then chuckled slightly. "I just can't understand why Odin refuses to listen to what the Ancients have told us."

"It may not have turned out the way you wished. But he does have a point. Without evidence there is nothing to go along with in this instance."

"Our very realm of life could be at risk of destruction at any moment and that old man refuses to listen to reason."

"Our realms are not threatened at this time. There is no

reason to raise alarm when there is no threat. He was just being concerned that you may not be thinking straight as you've been haunted by your own fear of this shadow for too long."

Athena walked over and took Zeus's hand; he looked up at her. "There may be hints that rise up with time, but for now we shouldn't worry about what the future holds. It can be rewritten an infinite number of times before it happens. No one knows with one hundred percent certainty what the future will hold. We may have already stopped this darkness before it's even surfaced."

Zeus took a breath as he calmed down his nerves. His arms were tense. "It may still come to be."

"It may and it may not. We do not have control over the future. We only have here and now, what we do now controls the future. It's the will of nature and the universe. Even we as Gods cannot alter that."

Athena took Zeus and led him out of the hall towards the sky where the sun was gleaming down with pure white light. Zeus took another breath and relaxed in the glow of innocence as he let his worry beam out of his mind.

While Athena and Zeus were basking in the glory of the light above ground things were much darker in the world below. Within the underworld of the Egyptian lands the God of the deceased, Anubis, performed his daily duties of weighing the hearts of the dead upon the grand scale of Ma'At, the Goddess of justice and truth. Times of distance between the realms of earth had changed over time and now the Gods of earth worked in unison to maintain balance.

Anubis was paired with Hades as the judgement before

the dead. The two were the bringers of death and the final judgement for all those who passed away. Anubis was the justice while Hades was the punishment. Within his realm Anubis stood before Ma 'At with two rivers by his side. These rivers, one for those hearts of purity which shine with light when deposited and one of shadow where the wicked and sinister are sent, are the final place that souls are placed before they enter their eternal resting place. The souls are contained within the hearts of the dead for that is the vehicle of life.

Those whose hearts are pure are placed within the flow of life where the soul is released and sent to Olympus to join Zeus and his family in light, the Egyptian souls joined Ra. Those whose hearts are evil and sinister are placed in the river of shadow; from there they go to the Underworld to await eternal suffering and pain from Hades, truly evil hearts were eaten by Anubis as fuel for his own strength. Only Anubis could touch the hearts of the deceased and he entrusted the judgement of the souls within to the Goddess of Ma'at who held the seven items of truth.

These items, forged by the Egyptians long before their civilization even began, were the key to the true nature of the race of man. The eye of truth upon Ma'at's forehead could view into the hearts of man and see their soul as white or dark. The key in her left hand unlocked the mind and allowed to user to enter the labyrinth of the human personality. Within her right hand she held the scales of truth and balance. These are what Anubis used to gauge the judgement of the dead. If the weight of the heart exceeds that of Ma 'At then the soul within is judged as evil and is sent to Hades down the river of death. Those which do not alter the scales against Ma'at's movements are judged as pure and join the river of light. While the scales judge, the eye seeks truth which is unlocked through the key. These items together create justice for the dead; as they see the mortal for how they truly lived.

Having already weighed several dozen hearts earlier that day, Anubis decided to take a break and sit down beside the river of souls. Ma 'At decided to rest as well for she needed a rest from the evil within most of the hearts she had already judged; and more were still pouring in, hearts of dread and villainy.

Taking a seat beside Anubis she asked, "What was the fate of the meeting you attended?"

"It was shorter than I anticipated it would be. Odin appeared quite certain his way is always correct." Anubis answered back in a sour tone.

"What was the outcome and reason behind that meeting?"

"I never told you?"

"You said you were forbidden to speak of it before it occurred."

"Right" Anubis said biting his own tongue. "The brothers Zeus, Poseidon and Hades were shown a vision long ago by ones they call The Ancients."

"The Ancients?!"

"You know of them?" Anubis quickly turned to face his jackal head towards his companion in disbelief.

"I know they are wise and powerful, wiser than anyone alive, if they showed the brothers a vision it must have been one of great concern."

ANGEL OF DARKNESS

"How wise are they, who are they?"

"They came before all of us. Born from the universe itself. Only stories and legends are heard of them, but it is said that they were greater than even the titans themselves."

"Those beasts were mighty indeed. But that does not answer my question. Who are The Ancients?"

"No one knows for sure, all we know is that they left behind great treasures of wisdom, it is said they live within the many worlds all at once and can see all things past, present, and future."

"Why have I never heard of these beings or their remains?" Anubis growled beginning to lose his temper.

"Their remains are well guarded secrets that only the wisest of beings are allowed to know about. But that is not important; what is important is what the Greek brothers were shown. Did they speak of it?"

"They did long ago it has become a faint memory in my mind, but it still remains. They were each shown what they assumed was their fate, their worlds being destroyed by a shadow of great power."

"That is unheard of." Ma 'At said as her face showed great concern.

"How do you know about The Ancients?" Anubis asked eager to hear her reply.

"They crafted these for the one who came before me." Ma 'At replied; shaking several of the items that were in her hands and around her neck.

"They crafted those items!?"

"Yes, now if you'll be quiet for a moment, I wish to gain

some enlightenment on this matter that the brothers faced." Ma 'At said as she closed her eyes and activated the power of the necklace around her neck.

Anubis remained silent; whenever Ma 'At wanted to gaze into the past with that neckless it was very unwise to disturb her. The last poor soul who tried that was banished to a realm of darkness and horror said to be the deepest darkest place within the Underworld itself. And the Underworld was very deep indeed.

The Ancient crafted those items? They were powerful beings indeed.

Several minutes passed as Anubis gazed over the hearts they still had to weigh. One heart he remembered was from a human said to be so terrible he plunged the entire world into utter chaos. When he had placed the heart on the scale not only did the scale fall instantly from the immense weight but Ma 'At went down with it. The heart was so evil Anubis had to devour part of it himself before Ma 'At could even move enough to activate the power of all seven of her items to regain her strength. That heart was sent to The Underworld without a second thought. Whoever was within; both beings hoped they were receiving punishment from Hades in ways far beyond death.

Ma 'At returned and stood up and Anubis gazed up at her. He saw a face of question gazing off into the cavern.

"What did you see?" Anubis asked, his voice low.

"I saw the Greek brothers descend into the lower levels of Olympus where they were shrouded by barriers they had created; I was forbidden to pass through, so I waited within the vision."

ANGEL OF DARKNESS

"What happened when they returned?"

"Their faces were full of fear and their breaths were deep and heavy. Something had disturbed them beyond reckoning."

"It must have been that vision they were shown, did they say anything?"

"No, they remained silent as they continued up to the surface."

"If it was The Ancients who showed them that vision, it must have been something to be able to scare them like that."

"What did Odin think of what the Gods said at your meeting?'

"Odin does not believe in what they saw. He believes that without proof there is no cause for alarm."

"Then he is a fool."

"What do you mean?"

"As legends say; The Ancients have never been wrong when it came to showing the fates and futures of others. While the future can change with even the slightest alteration of the past; if The Ancients predicted it then it will happen."

"What can we do?"

"We have to-AAAHHCCCKK!"

"Ma 'At? What's wrong?" Anubis cried as he rose to his feet, then he felt a presence passing overhead. Looking up he saw nothing but stone. Turning back to Ma 'At he saw something. The Scales of Balance were unable to find balance. They kept tilting and never stood still. Anubis called upon his dark magic to calm their motion, but it was no good. The power contained within them was stronger than anything he could conjure up. Ma 'At kept screaming for several minutes until finally she stopped. Looking at the scales, which stopped shortly after that, she turned to Anubis with great concern in her eyes.

"How long have the scales been unbalanced?!" Ma 'At asked quickly.

"What just…"

"HOW LONG!?"

"About ten minutes." Anubis cried taking a step back.

Ma 'At took a deep breath before turning towards the jackal. "Only something of great evil could cause the scales to be unable to find balance for that long. A darkness that knows no bounds."

"Could it be connected to the figure we just discussed?"

"That is the only thing that makes sense in this situation. Did anything happen while the scales' power was unleashed?"

"I felt something above us, but I saw nothing."

"There was something close, something powerful. What it was we may never know until time shows it."

"What must we do?"

"Wait for time to tell us more is the only thing we can do." Ma 'At said as she stood up and walked back to her place between the soul rivers. Anubis agreed with her for now; not once did he question her judgement. But something dark had passed over his gaze and he was positive the Greek Gods would want to hear of that soon.

ANGEL OF DARKNESS

"Only time will tell" he said to himself as he picked up a heart from the now twice as large pile they had begun earlier that day. "Are you sure you want to continue with this work? You can barely stand as it is?"

"I'm fine, let's just finish this day's load." Ma'at replied.

"If you say so then I believe you" Anubis said.

As he placed the heart on the scales, they instantly dropped. Ma'at quickly fell with them.

"Ma'at" Anubis cried out.

Her pale skin had gone even paler, and she had stopped breathing. Anubis quickly released a large level of energy into her body which was enough to wake her temporarily. "My strength is gone" she cried before falling silent. She was still breathing. Anubis decided to carry her to her chambers for rest; he kept releasing small amounts of his own strength to keep her alive. He knew the Olympian Gods would want to hear about this, and he also knew that something had passed overhead, something powerful.

Chapter Eight

YUKO WALKED ALONG the sidewalk towards the school shivering as she tried to stay warm. There was a mountain of snow that had fallen the previous night, so it was exceedingly difficult to move through. Behind her there were some snowplows going down the road trying to move what they could off to the side of the road so cars could still get past. Luckily, they had already run through the school areas, so it was easy for the bus to move once it got out of the deep white powder. Yuko was thankful that her family had come prepared with thick winter clothing but even layered down; Yuko could still feel the wind claw at her body. Winter in Canada was nothing to laugh at when you experienced it for yourself.

MICHAEL MCGEE

The air was chilly, and the wind only made it worse. It was funny. How when the wind died down the weather became nice and not the frozen state it was known for. Once the wind came in however it was an instant call to bundle up and try to stay out of the wind as much as possible. The wind wasn't the only problem; the fresh amount of snow that had fallen was being blown wildly and only made vision that much harder to focus on. Yuko felt like she was just released from prison when she finally made it into the school. The warm air instantly rushed the cold chill out of her flesh. Walking into the core area she saw that many students were stuck to the chairs as they tried to stay warm.

Even the people who have lived here all their lives still don't adapt very well to the cold.

She shivered from the sudden rush down her spine as the wind howled behind her.

Well, no time to be too concerned about the cold. If I want to try and help Max with whatever her past is, I have to start with information.

She walked over to a table close to the entrance and saw three guys who were all drinking a hot beverage. She recognized one of them as Michael, the one who helped her in science class when she fell asleep.

"Hey Michael," She said, trying not to let her shiver take over her words.

"Oh, hey Yuko, how are you doing?" He asked, his words also slightly obscured by the cold clicking in his teeth.

"I'm doing alright, thanks for your help the other day."

"No worries. So, how's the winter for you?"

ANGEL OF DARKNESS

"Cold very cold."

"Yeah, it's a bit different here than in Japan I bet, that is where you're from right?"

"Yes, that is where I'm from."

"Oh, good" Michael said with a sigh "I was worried that if you weren't from there it would be really embarrassing for me to ask that."

"That's alright," Yuko said with a small laugh to which the other two guys at the table laughed in unison.

"Oh, these are my friends David and John." Michael quickly said as the other two waved over at Yuko.

"Nice to meet you two, I'm Yuko."

"David" said the one in the red coat.

"John," followed the one wearing a blue coat that looked like it was for skiing. "Mike here was just telling us about how you passed out in science class the other day."

"I was not!"

David and John laughed at Mike's quick outburst. Yuko turned slightly red from embarrassment.

"Yeah" she said quietly. "Of course, he was."

"No, I was not!" Mike quickly replied.

All four of them looked at each other in unison before all bursting out laughing.

"Why are we laughing at this?" Mike asked as he tried to catch his breath.

"Your overreaction to what we said" replied David quickly.

MICHAEL MCGEE

"So, hey Michael" Yuko said once they calmed down.

"Call me Mike, it's just easier and that's what everyone calls me anyway."

"Ok Mike, I wanted to ask you something."

"If it's about me talking about you falling asleep in class, that was not me, John here happens to be in the same class as us."

"No, I wanted to ask you about Max. Do you know her?"

When she said that all three guys looked at each other. For a moment no one talked.

"I don't really know much about her. She keeps to herself most of the time." Mike quietly replied, turning back to Yuko. "Why do you want to ask about her?"

"She seems to be someone different to everyone here and she's not the same person who I've come to know over these past few weeks. So, I was wondering if you knew anything about why that is."

"All I can tell you is that she wasn't always like how she is today."

"Why is that?"

"It's a bunch of rumors that no one really knows if they are true or not, but they have stuck around and now everyone thinks the same of her." John said in a low voice.

"Why do you all sound scared?" Yuko asked quietly.

"No one really likes talking about what happened to her. Because we don't know the entire truth about what happened, we don't really want to get involved" Mike explained. "We try to stand out as people who try to help others, but there are some here who would take the stories

ANGEL OF DARKNESS

about Max and turn them against her."

"Like the Sisters?" Yuko questioned.

"Yeah, those three would definitely be the type of people who would use those rumors as power over the one they affected most." Mike replied.

"But like John said we don't know the truth, so we try to avoid it all together. I've talked to Max on several occasions, and she does seem like a nice person." David followed.

"Does she ever want to talk about her past?" Yuko asked.

"No, it's never been brought up whenever we talk." David said.

"Well how do you guys see her, like what kind of person is she?"

"She's nice and really smart," John said.

"And she's really good in construction class, I'm making the same bookshelf as her and she is way ahead of everyone else who are building one." David followed.

"Those are how we see her; if I were you Yuko, I wouldn't try to be bothered too much about what happened to her. Try to see her for who she is now and not focus on who she once was." Mike replied in a bit of a soothing voice.

"That seems like a good idea. But at the same time, I want to know what hidden side of her is seen by the other students here. Sorry I'm the kind of person who wants to help others as well and I need to understand them to be able to help them." Yuko replied calmly.

"Well why not try asking her yourself about what she faced when she was younger?" David suggested. "If you want to know her past then try asking her directly."

"I don't know how I should ask her." Yuko replied, "She gets worried whenever it's brought up in any way."

"That might be the only way you can get the answer you're looking for." John said as he got up. "Class is about to start however so we should probably get going."

"That is a good idea, I cannot afford to be marked late again" David said as he bolted up. "It was nice to meet you Yuko and good luck with trying to help Max." He bolted down the hall after he said that.

"Don't worry too much about it Yuko" Mike said as he grabbed his bag. "If you want to know then just try asking, nothing can go wrong with simply asking a question." With that he walked off and up the stairs as the bell rang. John ran off after him leaving Yuko by the table. She decided that she would try asking Max about her past the next time she saw her.

The bell had rung so Yuko grabbed her bag and headed off to her math class. When she got into the classroom she saw Max sitting at her desk looking at her notebook. Yuko walked over and saw that she was trying to figure out a long division question.

"You alright Max?" she asked as she sat down on her desk behind Max. She didn't answer. Yuko gently tapped her shoulder and she jumped. Rather suddenly.

"Sorry," Yuko said as Max quickly spun around.

"Oh, it's you,"

"You alright?"

"Yes, I'm fine" Max said taking a breather. "I'm just really

ANGEL OF DARKNESS

stuck on this last question from last night's assignment, and I can't figure it out."

"Long division?"

"Yeah, how did you know?"

"I saw them over your shoulder when I sat down. I'm stuck on them also." She had been up all night trying to solve the problem.

"Want me to help you?" Max asked.

"Sure, it's the fifth one that is difficult for me; I can't get the right answer." Yuko turned her notebook around so Max could scan over the question.

"Here's the problem" she said a minute later. "You've got the correct common denominator, but you haven't reduced it to its lowest possible form."

Yuko looked and sure enough Max was right. Just a simple reduction issue that she had completely overlooked. "Wow how did I mess that up?" she said as she reduced it two more times. Checking the back of the book where the answers were, she saw that her answer matched that which was on the last few pages.

"Small things like that are usually easily to overlook" Max explained. Her face suddenly changed to a form of realization "hang on." She turned back to her notes before bursting out "Idiot!"

"Who?" Yuko asked.

"Me, you're not the only one who overlooks small mistakes." Max said as she turned back to her own notes and scribbled frantically.

"What do you mean?"

"Half of these questions involve inverting the division into multiplication. But this last question has several symbols already in multiplication, so they don't need to be inverted." Max turned around and showed Yuko. There were three multiplication symbols mixed into the division symbols between the fractions they had to divide.

Max turned her textbook to the 'answers' section. "Got the right answer" she said.

"Good job." Yuko replied.

"Very good indeed" a third voice followed.

Yuko and Max turned to see the math teacher, Mrs. Lillis, standing beside them with a smile. "I'm glad you were able to figure out the answer."

"Thanks, but I did have some help." Max said nodding in Yuko's direction.

"All I did was make you realize you had overlooked a small mistake after you already pointed out that I had done the same." Yuko said.

"Well, it worked" Max said.

"Alright class time to get started today" Mrs. Lillis said as she moved to the front of the room. "Before we start, I want to point out an important point that Max and Yuko just realized themselves. Make sure you read over the question and your work slowly and several times. It is easy to miss small details that make the difference in the final answer."

Both girls turned away as most of the students glanced in their direction.

"I thought all Max did was cause problems, not solve

ANGEL OF DARKNESS

them," Yuko faintly heard one of the girls to her right say to the girl before her.

"What's that supposed to mean?" Yuko said louder than she wanted too. Several students near them heard and glanced back towards them.

"It's nothing" the girl said turning towards her.

"That didn't sound like nothing" Yuko replied quietly.

"Don't worry about it" the second girl said turning back to face the front.

"Why should I?"

"You don't know what she did before you came here, you're new so you don't understand. Now listen this is nothing you need to be concerned about so just stay out of it."

"Maybe you'd like to fill me in on the details?" Yuko said beginning to get tired of all the avoidance to her question.

"Pay attention back there" the teacher called out towards them. They all fell silent. The girl was smirking, Yuko was enraged.

Max was upset. She had heard what Yuko and Alexis were bickering about and she knew what Alexis had hid in all her words. She cringed as the memory rushed into her and her hands curled up, gripping the nervously filled air.

The class ended fifty minutes later. Max quickly rushed out of the room. Yuko heard her rush off and that reminded her that she wanted to ask Max about her past.

But would she want to talk now?

She decided to follow her and try asking at the least, but she quickly lost her in the sea of students. Finally making it into the construction room Yuko saw Max sitting in one of the work desks. She had already retrieved her bookshelf she had been working on for the last week and was now examining the wood that she needed to glue together for any imperfections. She didn't look up as Yuko approached.

"Hey Max, are you alright?" Yuko asked. Max didn't answer; she kept examining the wood as if she was a sculptor searching the slightest scratch in a statue. Yuko walked off into the storage room, deciding it wasn't the best time to ask her question, and retrieved her work. Laying her work on the workbench she retrieved the layout from her binder and examined what she needed to do next in making her table. She had to construct the legs next, which needed to be 24 inches long by 4 inches wide.

"I know what you want to ask me." Max said now looking over her layout. "Trust me, if I did tell you, you'd probably run away and avoid me like everyone else already does."

Yuko looked up at her and she glanced in her direction. "Why would I do that?"

"Because everyone else does, I've grown accustomed to it anyway."

"I don't think I would."

"Yuko please, forget it. I don't want to talk about it right now alright?" Yuko remained silent.

They did not talk to each other for the rest of the class. Max cut out pieces for her shelves, trying to cut her past away with the wood. Yuko worked on marking the proper measurements for her legs.

The remaining hours of the day were quiet around the

school. There was almost a gloomy feel in the air. Yuko and Max wandered through the halls and just as Max said everyone seemed to move out of the way for some strange reason. Yuko simply followed Max through the halls as if there was a thick mist no one could get through. The only one who knew the correct path was Max.

Things around the school stayed that way for a while. The variation throughout the day only occurred within the classes; everywhere else followed a routine. One that centered on Max and those around her. Mainly Yuko, with the odd exception of Megan and Alex on small occasions. Max moved through it as if she'd walked that path her whole life. Yuko slowly became distant from the other students. Everyone she approached turned away in rejection. Almost as if she contained a plague.

Yuko and Max seemed to slowly become the two students everyone else feared and no one wanted to talk about why it was like that. The only one who knew the truth was Max, and Yuko sensed getting the answer was not going to be easy.

Chapter Nine

YUKO WALKED ALONG the streets of town, alone, wondering what she was doing. She wanted to know the truth, but she did not know about how she would go about learning it. She could just ask Max directly; no, she would never get the answer openly from her because she doesn't want to talk about it.

"Maybe I could ask around the school. No that won't work because Mike said no one knows the truth, it's a bunch of circulated rumors."

She cried in frustration. She began running through thoughts that ranged from asking the locals if they knew anything to the insane idea to asking The Sisters for the answers.

She pulled out her phone and plugged in her earphones. She hit shuffle and a soft piano song came on, she immediately recognized it as Homura by LiSA. A sad song about saying goodbye, while moving forward at the same time. Yuko smiled as the vocalist's soft voice moved through her bones. It relaxed her.

She walked along letting the calm music guide her movements. The song changed, becoming more powerful, crying out against the pain of loss. The feeling of pushing forth. The struggle one feels as they continue. Eventually Yuko lost herself and unknowingly walking up to Max's front door. Staring at the door only taunted her desire to know the truth about her friend. She was about to knock when the door flew open and Max walked out, almost knocking Yuko over.

"Oh, Yuko what are you doing here?" Max asked.

"I'm not sure about that myself" she said as she removed her earphones.

Max stood still, "okay; that's odd."

"I guess"

"I'm going out to run some errands, want to come? Might help your mind figure out what's going on."

"Sure, if you don't mind."

"Come on then" Max said as she started down the street with Yuko rushing to catch up to her. They walked in silence for a while before Max asked, "How have you been recently?"

"I've been alright I guess."

"You guess?"

ANGEL OF DARKNESS

"I've just been thinking a lot recently."

"What about?"

"Are you going to keep asking that until I tell you?"

"Pretty much, so come on out with it."

Yuko took in a deep breath, trying to calm her nerves, before asking "Ok, here it is. What happened when you were younger? I'm only asking because everyone around us seems to see us as different. I… I can't hold back who I am and who that is someone who wants to try to help you because you are a different person whenever your past comes up and it's not the same person I see and know."

The trees around them swayed in the wind as she said that. Yuko felt the strange feeling from the other day return to her. Almost as if the town was trying to tell her now was the time to get the answer she was so concerned about. Max stopped walking and Yuko turned around to face her. She saw a blank face looking back at her.

"Who is the person you see now?" Max asked slowly.

"I see the same person I've known for these past few weeks. The same person who has become one of my best friends I've ever had. Only there's another side of you I can't see, and it's scary."

Max let out a small sigh; as if she knew that would be Yuko's answer. "Alright follow me" she said and started off towards the nearby forest. Yuko followed closely behind.

Max followed a trail through the woods that carried them up into the mountains. Yuko became slightly nervous. Max turned off the trail and climbed up a steeper hill. The snow on the ground made the climb difficult but both girls kept going. After about five minutes they emerged from the

MICHAEL MCGEE

trees and Yuko's mouth dropped.

Mountain peaks glistening in the white sun, blue sky far above them, a complete valley of trees and nature below them where the town could be seen within the vastness of tree lines. A river flowed off to the west from a mountain side, water fresh from the mountain peaks swirling with the wind. The wind whisked the snow and cold air around them on a different manner than down below where rivers of snow could be slightly seen gliding over the town. The wind was still cold but held a slight calmness and carried a subtle feeling of freedom with it.

Looking around she saw Max clearing snow off a log before sitting down, beckoning Yuko to do the same. Once they were both seated; Max looked down over the cliff. Silence descended on them for a minute, and then Max spoke.

"It was about two years ago, when I was about 14 years old. It was a cool fall day; leaves were changing color and the wind became brisk. I was at home having a good time with my father. We were relaxing, watching our favorite show, enjoying the day. Then the doorbell rang. My father went upstairs to see who it was while I waited on the couch. Then I heard yelling, and something hit the floor above me. I quietly went upstairs and looked around the corner only to see my father on the ground. A tall man was standing over him constantly kicking him. My father got up and fought back unaware that I was watching behind him. Then the intruder kicked my father's legs out from under him and slammed him into the ground. Then he pulled out a gun and aimed it at my father's back. He shot him right in his spine. Blood covered the floor as my father screamed in pain. I couldn't hold back my own scream. The man heard it and then saw me. As he walked towards me my father grabbed him by the ankle and pulled him down. The gun flew out of the man's hand and landed right in front of me. Out of fear I grabbed it and pointed it at the intruder. That didn't stop him from trying to get to me. I couldn't control my fear. Before I could stop myself, I shut my eyes and pulled the trigger. The gun kicked back and threw me against the wall. When I opened my eyes all I saw was a face filled with rage. With a small hole in his forehead. The man fell to the ground as I took a breath, the adrenaline just shot through me that I didn't feel anything."

"After a moment when I finally looked down at the blood on my hands, the gun in my fingers, the fear on the still pulled back trigger. I screamed at what I had done. I ran to my father who was still on the ground. He told me to call the police and the hospital, to tell them there was an intruder and nothing more. I did what he told me while crying the entire time. When the police and medical team arrived, they took my father and me out of the house and took us to the hospital. My father survived however he lost the use of his legs for good. He told them what happened. He left out the part about me killing that man. The police ruled it as self-defense during an armed robbery, so no charges were placed on my father."

"The news said it as an armed robbery gone wrong and that my father was the one who pulled the trigger. I still don't know how; but the truth got out. Everyone in my school knows it was me who pulled the trigger and that I was always stunned by what I had done. That's why they are afraid of me and why they constantly taunt me about it."

Max took a breath before finishing "So now you know

about me and why everyone who sees me runs away. If you wanted to you could do the same. I won't stop you."

After she finished Max held her head on her shoulders. Yuko sat there beside her. She never imagined Max's past would have been that extreme. Now that she knew about it, she could feel some part of her wishing she didn't.

"Is your father alive?" Yuko asked after a few minutes.

"Yes, he's fine, paralyzed from the waist down, but otherwise alright."

"What about you?"

Max looked up to face Yuko in the eyes. "I'm struggling to forget it ever happened."

"Maybe this is something you can't forget."

"What do you mean?"

"It sounds like this is an experience that shouldn't be forgotten. Like the more you try and forget about it, the stronger the memory becomes."

"But I want to forget it; I want the pain to go away."

"How long have you been trying to forget?"

"Ever since it happened those jerks at school who know about it keep bringing it up, which makes it impossible for me to stop thinking about it."

"You mean The Sisters?"

"Them and a few others. Most people are too afraid of me to say anything directly towards me, but I know they talk about it when they think I can't hear them."

"I don't talk about you behind your back."

"But you do talk about me; I overheard you and Alexis

ANGEL OF DARKNESS

in math the other day."

"That was a situation that presented itself that one time. I don't talk about you in negative ways though." Max hung her head in disagreement. "Neither do Megan or Alex."

"Megan and Alex?" Max said with a glance at Yuko.

"They both have been trying to be friends with you for a while now, why do you think they join our conversations during the lunch break and after school?"

"They were pretending. Come on you saw how they reacted when you first met them, and they saw me."

"Recently they've been trying to get better acquainted with you; you just don't see it yet."

"Because they know what I did so they want to try and cheer me up?"

"Because you've shut yourself within your past and you don't see when people are being friendly and compassionate towards you. So, you killed a person when you were young, you're a different person because of that and it's someone who I see as a good friend."

Max looked up.

"Friend?" She asked.

"Of course, you're the first person I met since I moved here; you've shown me around this town and also this amazing secret view of yours."

"I was just being friendly."

"Well, it was enough for me. The person I know isn't a murderer. She's a person who is kind and wants to have a life where she doesn't have to worry anymore."

Max stared. She didn't know what to say. All her life she had shut herself within the horrible deed she had done when she shot that man. Everyone around her afterwards avoided her like the plague and she drifted off into a corridor of loneliness. All that and yet here was someone who, even after learning the truth, didn't run or taunt her. There was something unique to Yuko that made her one of the best friends she had ever had. Yuko was right that she never noticed it until now.

"Thanks Yuko, you're a great friend as well" Max said with a smile.

"There's the smile you've hid from everyone. What do you saw we go run those errands we've put off for the last hour and then we can put this bad memory behind us once and for all?" Yuko said.

"Great idea" Max said. With that the two friends walked back down the hill as the rays from the sun illuminated the snow below them.

"Hey, I why did you take me there to tell your story?"

"That's a location I discovered one time while hiking around here. Kept it a secret ever since. I go there frequently to rest my nerves and try to forget."

"Why did you show it to me?"

"Because it's the only place where I can think about my past. It's the place I find the most peace, so it's more…"

"Forgiving?"

"Yeah…forgiving."

Chapter Ten

HADES WALKED THROUGH the doors to his castle within the Underworld. The words that Odin spoke to him, and his brothers still ate away at his sanity. The words of Anubis didn't help the situation either, "that damn jackal headed fool" he said out loud as he paced his chambers. There was a being of darkness out there somewhere he was sure of it. Hades sat down on a chair as he tried to calm his throbbing mind. Something didn't feel right. He felt as if something was out of place. Hades focused his mind on the entities within his domain; he saw several souls screaming in terror and pain, hundreds more burning within fields of fire. Nothing out of the ordinary, except for a small group of souls rushing towards the exit caverns.

"Maybe I'll go have some fun" Hades thought aloud, it had been a while since he personally tortured the dead and thought it would be a good way to change his mood.

"Everything alright?"

Hades looked up and saw Persephone standing in the entrance to his chambers. A pomegranate held softly in her hand.

"I'm fine my sweet, just thinking about how to pass the time."

"Well, I'm sure you'll figure something out."

"Winter has dawned upon the mortal realm early this year, I was not expecting you to be back so soon."

Persephone smirked, "I am forever bound to you."

Hades smirked back.

"I'm going to rest in my chambers, do not wake me," Persephone said before she retreated. Hades returned his attention to the souls of the Underworld.

"Time for some fun."

Rushing out of his castle Hades flew over the pillars of fire towards the caverns. He soon saw the souls rushing towards the exit; they couldn't escape as long as the gate was up, so they were only running towards a dead end. Their green bones glowed in the dark area surrounding them. There were four of them and they moved in unison, almost as if trying to avoid separation. They were like a flock of birds flying in the wind, carrying each other on the slipstream that the leader provided. When Hades approached them, the souls screamed in terror, but only for a second, then they calmed down.

ANGEL OF DARKNESS

Hades looked at them for a second. Souls that were not scared of their eternal ruler. That was something that had never happened before. All the souls that came into The Underworld looked away in fear the instant Hades ever glanced over them. But these souls just stared back. Hades stared at them, and they at him. Then one soul looked over its shoulder and shrieked in such a way that the other souls instantly turned around as well, all of them screamed and increased their speed. Hades looked back and saw something chasing them, another soul, but not from this realm. Most of the souls glowed with a green aura from the radiation that deteriorated from their bones after they died. This soul didn't have any bones. It didn't have any form at all. It was just a dark shadow. The green souls turned down a second corridor while Hades stopped and stared at the shadowy being which had also stopped its approach.

The two beings stared at each other; neither one making a move. The shadow before him swayed in the dim light from the flaming abyss.

"What are you?" Hades asked without taking his gaze off the being.

There was no answer. The being swayed as if observing him. Then the shadow dashed down the corridor adjacent to the two beings and was swallowed by the darkness.

Hades rushed after the soul as it tried to escape through the caverns. Melting from his body his soul dashed forward at increased speed. The shadow was fast and evasive. It moved through the walls with amazing speed. Hades sent out a shroud of souls from his own body to corner the target. The souls all separated and struck at every angle in front of the target, the shadowy form halted. As the souls and Hades came within arm's length the shadowed figure dashed upwards and out of their reach as the souls all collided in a fury of screams. Hades lost vision of the figure for he could not see it through the dark walls of The Underworld and the mist of the colliding souls. Hades was shocked.

As he returned to his body, a whining sound echoed against the chasm. Moving down the corridors he saw Cerberus by the river of souls, he was cowering. His paws were over his heads which were buried in his fur. As Hades approached Cerberus cowered even more, something had frightened him. That was impossible. Cerberus is not afraid of anything; nothing has ever scared him in the past. Hades thought it was that being he just lost in chase. What was that thing that could make the most feared creature of the Underworld cower in fear?

Hades sat beside Cerberus. He was confused and furious at the same time. Something had entered his realm and he had no knowledge of it. That was impossible. There was only one passage into this dark realm, and it was protected by not only Cerberus but also the gate that Hades designed himself.

The gate

Hades thought for a second before rushing down the corridor to it. Examining every inch of it he found no alteration or temperance of either the metal or the dark shroud which surrounded its bars. Staring at the gate Hades thought; how?

How was this shadowy being able to through this aura?

Phasing from his body Hades separated his soul from his body. Meditating like this was risky as it left his true spirit vulnerable to attacks, but it was also how he could search every section of the Underworld and analyze every soul within it at once. Hades scanned the darkest pits to the near surface of the mortal world above.

Nothing.

Hades sensed nothing that matched the shadow that had just evaded him. How was that possible unless the being already made it into the mortal realm? No there is no way to exit this realm other than through this tunnel. So how is this shadowy being unexpectedly gone? Hades' rage filled his soul as much as these unanswered questions tormented him. Returning to his body he rose and stood against the cavern walls. Cerberus came around the corner a few moments later. His heads still showed fear. Hades took that into consideration as he thought of all possible explanations. All his thoughts came to the same conclusion, the being that the Ancients had shown him and his brothers.

If that was the case, then what would my brother's think? They had both been struck by Odin's words about our vision being false.

"No, I know my brothers; they won't be swayed so easily by that old man. Perhaps Chiron can provide some insight towards this strange being. I don't think it would help my brother's mindset if I tell them what has occurred without first being absolutely sure of my own opinions." Hades said as Cerberus came and sat down beside his master.

The two waited for several minutes in silence. Then Cerberus's heads jumped up and his ears straightened, looking up Hades saw Chiron approaching. Black robes and hood covering his dead nature as he rowed his boat full of chained souls towards the gate of the Underworld.

"Hades it has been a while since I last saw you near this side of the Underworld." Chiron spoke in a deadly tone.

"Tell me Chiron has a dark shadow passed your gaze recently?" Hades asked quickly.

"No great one, no such being has passed my gaze." Chiron replied as his red eye glared at his master. "The only things that have come to my eyes are beings such as these" he pointed to the souls who began screaming.

"How many trips have you made today to the Underworld?"

"I have made two trips with the dead today. Why do you ask such questions?"

"Because a dark shadow just evaded me, and I wish to know more about it."

"A dark shadow, that could resemble anything my lord, would you mind being more descriptive of this lost soul you seek knowledge of?"

"I never said it was a soul."

"That is all that passes through the Underworld these days. What else could it be?"

"I don't know. All I know is that I felt something when chasing a few souls through the passages and then I saw a dark shadow behind me. I didn't know what it was, but I know it was not natural to this place. I pursued this intruder, and it evaded me with its extreme speed and cunning. It was smart. Moments later I found Cerberus in a state of fear."

"Fear?" Chiron asked loudly to which Cerberus growled in response. "What could possibly scare the hound of

ANGEL OF DARKNESS

Hades?"

"I don't know, but this being seems to have escaped somehow. I was unable to sense it after I lost sight of it."

"That is strange. There is no other way out of these lands except through this passageway behind me. So how could something just disappear?"

"As I said I do not know."

As Hades and Chiron began to think about what the answer to these new questions could possibly be; the souls which were still chained to the boat began to scream louder for freedom.

"Arg. I can't think with those fiends screaming like banshees. Come on through and Cerberus can take them from here."

"That sounds like a great idea," Chiron screamed as he covered his hood trying to drown out the screams.

Hades raised his hand and the gates to the Underworld creaked open. When Chiron docked his boat the souls crept towards the three headed dog who glared over them with all three rows of teeth exposed. As Hades was about to close the gate, he felt a chill rush past him, coming from the Underworld. Looking back, he saw that both Cerberus and the chained souls had stopped and were all looking down into the dark abyss before them.

"Shut the gate" Chiron said, also frozen in place.

"What did you say?" Hades asked not taking his eyes off the darkness before him.

"SHUT THE GATE NOW" Chiron yelled in fear.

Hades turned his focus back to the gate as Cerberus

began barking and growling in a rampage towards the caverns. As the gates began to recede Hades felt something approaching. Fast. Turning his head Hades saw something rush down the corridor, a wave of energy preceding it. A loud shriek echoed through the caverns. Cerberus instantly stopped his rampage as the waves rushed over him; all his heads lowered their assault; his paws instantly covered his ears. A shadow rushed over the dog's heads towards the gate which was still open. Hades unleashed a wall of souls from his being, the sound that radiated off the walls made that process very difficult. The wall grew in height as souls climbed over each other, obeying their captives command, but the shadow was too quick. It glided over the wall of spirits and through the minute gape in the gate just as the gate closed behind it.

"That was it that was the shadow that evaded me moments ago!" Hades roared.

"It was here all along, waiting for the barrier to be lowered." Chiron followed gripping his staff for support.

"We have to go after it."

"Do not open the gate!"

"Why not?"

"It waited for the barrier to be lowered before escaping. Based on that we can assume it can't pass through it."

"That's helpful but at the same time we cannot let it escape."

"We do not know what this being was here for, so I suggest we wait."

"Wait?"

ANGEL OF DARKNESS

"Yes, for now we know that whatever that was is fast and powerful. More importantly we know this being or soul exists."

"That confirms my suspicions, something is rising, and I fear it is what I foresaw all those years ago. I must warn my brothers of this at once."

"I shall ensure the gate remains closed until you return."

"Thank you, and do not forget that shadowed being may return. For now, it is lost to the darkness." With that Hades opened a portal and stepped through it as he teleported himself towards Olympus.

Zeus sat down on his throne as he considered Athena's words. There may still be a being out there. The one thing that bothered Zeus the most was when this being would show itself. It had been over two thousand years and just as Odin has said there was no change in nature.

"Brother!!" a voice echoed through the chamber. Zeus looked up in surprise as a pillar of shadow and flame erupted from the center of the chamber. Zeus rose and called lightning to his side, ready to strike, but stopped when he saw Hades fly out of the pillar and land in front of him.

"Hades why are you-"

"Brother, I saw it!"

"Saw it?"

"The being from our vision, it was in the Underworld mere moments ago!"

"WHAT!?"

"At least I believe it was that being. I cannot be entirely

sure. But something was down there, something powerful."

"Hades calm down."

"How can I be calm when an unknown force not only evaded my grasp and escaped, but was also able to enter the Underworld in the first place?"

"HADES" Zeus roared shaking the chamber "CALM DOWN!"

Hades looked up and Zeus saw great concern within his face. After several minutes Hades relaxed his shoulders and took a breath.

"Alright?" Zeus asked.

"Yes, I'm calm now," Hades replied.

"Good, now you saw something in the Underworld?"

"Yes, and I believe it was the being that the Ancients showed all those years ago."

"How can you be so sure?"

"It was a figure enveloped in a dark mist. I have never seen such a being within the dead who have entered my realm before. Chiron claims he never saw such a being pass his gaze either. Not only was this being also able to evade us both, I was also unable to sense it within the Underworld in the first place."

"You were unable to sense a being within your realm?"

"I only sensed it when it approached, otherwise I could not detect it at all. I even shredded my body to open my mind to the entire Underworld and even then, I felt nothing."

"What about that gate of yours? Surely it should have

prevented this figure from moving through it?"

"I know it could not have passed through the gate. It escaped before the gate was closed so I assumed that it cannot pass through the barrier that protects it and my realm from intruders."

"While we are talking about this, I have been meaning to ask you, what powers that gate of yours? You mentioned it can disrupt energy around it, but how does that occur?"

"The power of the gate comes from energy once contained within a former servant of mine. To answer your second question the gate does not disrupt energy, it absorbs it and transfers that strength to a holding chamber I keep in the darkest levels of my castle. If needed I can gain a large amount of energy by absorbing the energy my gate has transferred to the chamber."

"You never mentioned a being worthy of serving under you, who is this being?"

"He was strong, so strong I began to fear his strength, and under that influence I banished him from my realm and my service."

"What was the name of this being?"

"I refuse to speak it! That being's power was so great I feared my own safety and swore I would never say that monsters name again with added hopes of never seeing him again."

"Also, when did you install that chamber under your castle and how much energy can one gain from it?"

"I installed the chamber before constructing the gate. As for the strength levels one can absorb from it, that varies depending on the strength of those who try to pass beyond the gate's field, stronger beings lose more energy, and thus more energy can be given to me. But enough of that; can we get back to the matter at hand. You know; dark being that just passed by my gaze?"

"Yes, forgive me; my curiosity often gets the better of me."

"That much is obvious most times" Hades replied to which Zeus' brows tightened in silent response.

"What else were you able to notice about this being?" Zeus asked returning them back to their current concern.

"Not much, but I know it came into the Underworld for a reason, what that reason is though I have not figured out. There was definitely something unsettling about this being as it was able to frighten Cerberus and calm his rampage almost instantly when it passed over and escaped."

"Frighten Cerberus, that three headed dog of yours that set my robes on fire?"

"Yes, that dog of mine" Hades said angrily. "Nothing has ever frightened Cerberus before, so it makes me more concerned than ever. Only something of pure darkness could have possibly scared Cerberus, if even slightly. The only other being that has been able to even make Cerberus flinch was that previous servant of mine."

"How is Cerberus now?"

"A bit on edge but otherwise he is alright."

"And the shadow escaped?"

"As I mentioned before, it escaped, and I have no idea where it has gone."

"Perhaps we should just leave it at that for now then? We

will just have to keep an eye out for anything that may point out its whereabouts."

"What do you suppose these signs might be?"

"Unnatural occurrences, dark auras appearing, I don't know. All I know is that something is out there, and we need to keep an eye out for it as this may be as you said the dark being from our vision."

"I guess for the moment that is all we can do. At least until we gain more-"

"ZEUS!!" a voice cried out before Hades could finish his sentence.

Hades and Zeus both turned to look towards the chamber entrance just as the door blasted open creating a crack in the air. A being stopped before the brothers as the air rushed forwards to catch up.

"Hermes?" Hades asked as his robe swept in the wind.

Hermes stood before the brothers. The wings on his shoes, helmet, and arm gauntlets fluttered with great intensity. "Hades" he said quickly "good this saves me a trip down to the Underworld as this concerns you too."

"What do you mean?"

"I bring word for you, Zeus and Poseidon from the Egyptian God of the dead Anubis."

"What does he say?" Zeus asked straightening his beard which had blown back into his face.

"Something has occurred within The Scales of Balance, and I need to speak to you about this matter immediately. Come to my realm as quickly as you can." Hermes replied.

"The Scales of Balance?" Zeus spoke suddenly.

"You know what those are?" Hermes and Hades asked in unison.

"I've only heard stories about them, but from what the stories tell, those are one of several items that the Egyptians guard with great secrecy. Have you informed Poseidon about this sudden need for our attendance?"

"Yes, I told him first before I came here" Hermes replied. "He was not happy with the waterspout I caused in the middle of the ocean in order to get his attention."

"He did not want you to wake the kraken before it had its one hundred years of rest" Hades replied. "I heard the last time that happened my brother was not pleased with the young mer-child who woke it up after getting too curious and exploring where she shouldn't have. It took Poseidon forever to calm the beast down, but not before it caused great damage to mortal ships and claimed many lives in the process of its massive rampage."

"Yes, Poseidon did mention that to me with his trident at my throat." Hermes replied.

"You two can talk all about that creature later. For now, let us focus on the events that we were just informed of and experienced." Zeus said.

"Wait, what else has occurred?" Hermes asked.

"Hades catch him up will you, I need to go talk to my brother about meeting with Anubis as he is surely currently occupied with his sleeping pet." With that Zeus crashed away in a bolt of lightning.

Hades and Hermes sat down and discussed the intruder within the Underworld while they waited for Zeus to return.

ANGEL OF DARKNESS

"Very strange" Hermes said when Hades finished. "Do you think this has anything to do with The Scales of Balance being disrupted?"

"Before you brought those up, I wasn't sure what to think. My first thought was that this shadow is connected to the dark being of death that my brothers and I were shown."

"That does seem to fit the circumstances of the situation so I would not call it a coincidence."

"Neither would I."

A crash sound outside was all the two Gods needed to know that Zeus had returned. When they walked outside, they saw Poseidon standing beside Zeus.

"Hey Poseidon" Hermes said with caution "nothing happened right?"

"You did not wake the Kraken" Poseidon said loudly "but next time just call out to me from the shores. Someone in the sea will hear it and let me know you want to talk to me."

"I understand"

"Well, that makes someone around here," Poseidon said with a glance towards Zeus. "That aside, I agree we should go and see what Anubis has to say, the only question I have is how are we going to enter Anubis' realm?"

Zeus, Hades, and Hermes looked at each other for a second. Anubis layered his realm with traps and only he could deactivate them.

"We enter by paying our respects to the dead of course." Hades said. "Is that now how he was able to tell you he wanted to see the three of us Hermes?"

"It was Sobek who relayed the message to me. I never entered Anubis' realm. Too many traps and to even get to them you face a massive labyrinth."

"Alright so can't we just ask Sobek to relay a message to Anubis about letting us enter without his traps?" Poseidon asked.

"That may work however I don't think Anubis will respond considering how protective he is over his realm" Hades replied.

"It may be worth a shot though don't you think?" Zeus said.

"I guess it couldn't hurt" Hades answered.

The brothers linked arms and prepared to teleport together to Egypt. "You may want to step back Hermes" Zeus suggested to which Hermes backed away quickly just before a wave of light struck the clouds as the Gods disappeared.

The bolt of lightning struck the earth with great intensity. Thankfully, no mortals were around the area and the Gods knew it would be easy to wipe the memories of anyone who spotted them, so they weren't worried. The Nile flowed quietly before them; patches as green as the trees which reflected off the blue water could be seen in the current. Poseidon tapped the water's surface with his trident and called out to Sobek with his mind. Several minutes passed before the waters parted and Sobek emerged, his crocodile scales shimmered with the water residue that stuck to his back.

"Poseidon, it's been a while since you came here to

ANGEL OF DARKNESS

Egypt," Sobek said with a growl in his voice.

"I've never had any reason to come to this desolate wasteland of heat." Poseidon replied towards the yellow eyed being.

"I assume your reason to come today is related to the message Anubis relayed to me."

"That is correct, we were wondering if you would be able to ask Anubis to disable his barriers which defend his realm so we may enter unscathed."

"I cannot" Sobek replied. "Anubis told me that he will keep his barriers up indefinitely after those secret scales of his acquaintance Ma'at were disrupted."

"Great, well then this was a waste of time." Zeus spoke getting annoyed with the resistance to their emergency. "So where is the entrance to Anubis' realm anyway?"

"Within the tombs of the pyramids of course" Hades answered to Sobek's open jaw as he was about to answer that himself.

Closing his jaw Sobek said "Good luck getting past his traps, Anubis is very clever. Not even I can pass through them unscathed" With that Sobek dove back into the Nile and swam away, his scales camouflaged him against the water's surface.

Chapter Eleven

ANUBIS WAS ONE of the most protective Gods known to man. He was the guardian of the great tombs of the ancient pharaohs and in his eyes, none must disturb the dead. That is what worried Zeus, Hades, and Poseidon. While they did have ties with the Egyptian Gods, Anubis was always a stricter individual and always kept his domain secure from intruders. As the Gods walked along the corridors within the pyramids, they were surprised at the level of opposition they faced. There was none. No mummies, no scarabs, nothing to thwart off intruders, just an endless labyrinth of dark corridors.

Hades led the way, as being the ruler of the dead meant he could sense the feeling of death within the tombs.

Following the strongest scents, they would reach Anubis. Along the way Hades informed Poseidon of the intruder to the Underworld. Poseidon agreed that something was amiss and was almost certain Anubis had some form of an answer to their questions.

After about an hour of walking the Gods reached a large open chamber. A maze of pathways extended over a dark abyss below. Statues of Egyptian palace guards were scattered along the walkway. Torches lit the areas making the path slightly visible, but it was still very faintly illuminated.

"The first test," Zeus said towards the darkness.

"It appears so," Hades coldly said as the air was well below the temperature of the world above. "We must tread this path carefully and we must abide by the Egyptian rules."

"Well then I guess you just volunteered to be the first to go," Poseidon said towards Hades who grunted in response to his brother's *smart* tactics.

As Hades stepped onto the walkway, he kept his mind open. Anubis was clever with riddling his traps, so there had to be a solution. As Hades walked towards the first statue, he noticed that it was holding two Khopesh, one in each hand. Peering past he saw that all the statues held two of these ancient weapons. As he proceeded, he stopped before the first statue, they had to be connected to the riddle in some way as they would not be here otherwise. As he stared, he noticed that the statue began to shiver. Hades had a moment's notice with which to back away as the Khopesh was swung at his body. The statue was moving towards him furiously swinging its arms. Hades quickly noticed all the statues were moving along the pathway which they were set upon. As he took another step back the statue instantly stopped moving. Glancing around he saw all the statues had stopped.

"Hades" Poseidon called.

"What is it?"

"The statues feet, look at them."

"Their feet?" Hades looked down at them, not moving his own. The feet of the statues looked like ordinary human feet. All the statues had the same feet and on all of them the left foot preceded the right.

The left foot. Looking at his own feet he saw they his left foot was ahead of his body just as the statue's feet were. "Brother you're a genius" he called back to Poseidon. Of course, that was the answer. The Egyptians always placed their left foot before them when approaching the Pharaoh as a sign of respect because the heart was located on the leftmost side of the body. So, to place your left foot ahead was also placing the heart towards the King of Egypt.

"I don't understand." Zeus said.

And he's supposed to be the wisest of the three of us. Hades thought. "Walk with your left foot forward." he called before proceeding making sure to keep his left foot ahead of him at all times.

Once they were all across the cavern Zeus turned to Poseidon and asked, "how did you figure that out?"

"Easy, while Hades was keeping his eyes on the weapons which tried to cut him in half, I was studying the statues design and looked for hints as to what they all shared in common. That's when I noticed how their feet mirrored

Hade's feet when he stopped moving and how the statues reacted."

"Come on you two we need to keep going" Hades said before his brothers could turn a small situation into something violent. They loved to argue and were well known to resort to fist fights when they disagreed. Why they always turned to violence for answers was always beyond Hades' understanding of his brothers.

The Gods continued down the passageways. Often straying into side corridors. Zeus began to question Anubis's sanity as to the depth they were going to reach him, and how deep into the earth he really had to construct his realm. Hades did not question it; the Underworld had caverns which descended into eternal darkness. That level was yet to be reached within these halls, so he knew they still had a ways to go.

After another long trek, the Gods arrived at another chamber. One with more lit than the previous one. Upon the walls were pictures depicting the different Gods of the Egyptians. The level of detail that went into these images was easily nothing compared to what some of the Gods could create, but one could not easily dismiss the amount of creativity that went into the carvings.

As the Gods reached the center of the chamber the door behind them shut. A red aura quickly enveloped the walls and ceiling. Zeus moved towards one of the walls and cautiously extended his hand. The result was scorching, literally, as soon as he contacted the aura his hand was burned and lit a blaze as he was blown back. Poseidon easily extinguished the flame with a blast of water from his finger, but the skin was still severely burned.

ANGEL OF DARKNESS

"Looks like we're trapped." Zeus said as his brothers helped him up.

"Well, I guess we have to look for more clues." Hades stated.

"Scan the walls, maybe they have an answer, just don't touch the barrier." Zeus suggested.

The Gods examined the walls carefully. Hades then noticed, along the wall opposite the one they entered, there were hieroglyphics which glowed golden against the red barrier. It took some time but eventually the Gods were able to decipher what the words said.

Great to Anubis

Father of the Earth

Birthed the stars and the sky

Appears when his father rises high

"A riddle," Hades said as he stared at the words.

"Great to Anubis," Zeus followed "could this be pertaining to a person?"

"Appears when his father rises high it must be a God," Poseidon said. "The paintings on the walls they're the clues."

While Hades and Poseidon scanned the walls looking for who the riddle was pertaining too, Zeus was focused on the riddle's words. All the clues linked to one answer, but the words contained within that answer didn't seem to be connected with a single God. "Someone who is the Father of the Earth? Poseidon who is the Egyptian God of Earth?"

"I believe that is Geb if I'm not mistaken."

"Then who is Geb's father?"

"That would be Ra wouldn't it?" Hades suggested.

"Ra is the father of Geb but that doesn't complete the riddle as he did not give birth to the stars and skies." Zeus told them.

"Ra matches the second line of the riddle but being that he is the King of the Egyptian Gods I don't think he would have a father." Hades replied.

"But he is the God of the sun, and the sun does rise high." Zeus stated.

"Then the answer has to be connected to someone who gave birth to the Earth God, Geb, as well as both the Gods of the stars and the sky." Hades stated.

"Perhaps," Poseidon said, "So who are the Gods of the stars and skies to the Egyptians?"

"Horus is the God of the sky I know that because he and I often have friendly competitions over who can travel fastest" Zeus said to which Hades and Poseidon laughed under their breaths. "Go ahead and laugh, but I know you often race through the oceans with some of your royal guards as a way to test them" Zeus said towards Poseidon.

"Before you two start fighting like you always do, can we figure out this riddle we are forced to face in order to see what Anubis wants to talk to us about, need I remind you about the dark force that opposes us for an unknown reason?" Hades yelled towards the two Gods who looked like they were about to turn this dorm of fire into a war zone between the two of them.

"We weren't going to start fighting" Poseidon told Hades "You're way too paranoid with that idea that every time we

ANGEL OF DARKNESS

talk, we will turn it into something destructive."

"Let's just focus on the task at hand." Hades replied.

The three sat down on the floor to calm down and try to figure out what the riddle's answer was. They were unable to find an answer to the God of the Stars.

"What if it is one God the riddle is referring too when it states, 'birthed the stars and the sky'?" Hades suggested.

"That could be something we can consider." Poseidon replied, "is there a God of the both the stars and sky?"

"There is" Zeus said, "Nut."

"So, then who is the father of Nut?" Hades asked.

It took a minute of thought but then the three had the answer "Shu!" they all said in unison.

As soon as they said the name the walls began to change. The aura changed from a dark red to a bright yellow. The brothers stood in the center of the room as they watched the light converge on a single point on the ceiling where a picture of Ra could be seen.

The eyes of the painted Ra glowed as the light moved towards them, a moment later the light shone from the eyes onto the wall where a picture of Anubis stood. The beams connected with Anubis's scepter and grew into an entryway. The aura expanded beyond the new entryway and generated a corridor. As the Gods stepped through it they stood in shock at their new surroundings.

A bridge of solid hard light spread over an abyss of utter darkness. Rivers of green and white currents could be faintly seen beneath the bridge. The light extended before the Gods where it declined towards a crack in a wall which was impossible to see if not for the bridge. As the brothers walked along their new walkway they could all sense the presence of death and decay. This was definitely the place for the dead to dwell. When they reached the walls at the end of the pathway, the Gods didn't see walls, but two statues. One of a man with the head of an eagle holding a scepter, the other a jackal headed man who held a staff.

"Ra and Anubis." Hades said as he stared at the statues remarking at the level of detail and accuracy in their depiction of the two beings. Passing between the statues the brothers continued onwards on the path before them. Several minutes passed before they entered a dimly lit dwelling, a cavern surrounded by stone. The only light which entered this cavern was reflected from the two rivers which flowed into the center of the room before splitting down separate paths. The Gods followed the rivers path until they heard sounds coming from the green river's path. They stopped and listened, and then they heard footsteps approaching. Standing in the darkness the Gods stared down the corridor of darkness as two emerald lights illuminated the shadows, a moment later Anubis appeared.

"Anubis." Hades said towards the being. Anubis looked up and gazed upon them, his emerald eyes shining in the shadows.

"It's about time you three showed up, what happened the kraken woke up again?" the jackal headed human said crossly.

"What are you talking about?" Poseidon asked "you're the one who decided to layer the path to your realm with traps. We were busy dealing with those."

"I figured you of all people would have no problem

ANGEL OF DARKNESS

getting passed them."

"Well, we don't really know too much about your ancestors" Zeus said, "so that last challenge took us longer than we wanted."

"Maybe you should try to get better knowledge of where we all come from." Anubis said as he barred his teeth.

"You can teach us all about that later, for now you called us here for a reason, what is it?" Hades said towards Anubis.

Anubis put his teeth away as he turned to the fellow God of death. "Yes, I did call you here, come with me." Anubis led the Gods down a corridor separate from the rivers. They emerged into a smaller room where Ma'at was lying down on a stone bed.

"What happened here?" Zeus asked when he saw Ma'at.

"Her power has been nearly drained completely. Several hours ago, something happened." Anubis explained as he walked over and took something that rested beside Ma'at. "Something disrupted the balance between these" he said as he turned back towards the Greeks holding a set of gold scales.

"The Scales of Balance, yes we know, Hermes informed us of your message." Hades spoke. "What we want to know is what could have caused this to occur and how? We've got our own problems that just emerged as a matter of fact."

"What has occurred for you?" Anubis asked.

"Tell us what you want to say and then we'll tell you what occurred," Hades replied.

"Very well, I believe the event containing the scales

being disrupted ties into that being you three spoke of at that meeting in Asgard." Anubis said.

"I thought you didn't believe in that being?" Poseidon asked.

"I didn't until this occurred. Only something of immeasurable evil and boundless darkness could have done this. Ma'at and I both used up a great level of strength to return the scales to a resting position; they were unbalanced in the likes I've never seen before." Anubis told the three brothers.

"Did you feel anything when this occurred? Anything that felt extremely powerful?" Hades asked.

"Yes, I did, there was a strong presence that I felt pass overhead." Anubis replied.

"If you looked up in response, did you see anything, mainly a dark shadowy form?"

"No, I saw nothing; I only felt an immense amount of power. Why did you ask for such a description?"

"Because something with that description just passed through and escaped the Underworld several minutes before we received your message." Hades explained.

"WHAT?!" Anubis screamed. Hades informed him. "That confirms my thoughts there is definitely something out there."

"How can you be so sure?" Poseidon asked.

"Think about it gill-brain. You three were shown a being made of shadow; the Scales of Balance are thrown off balance. Shortly after a being with immense power bearing that same description of a shadowed being enters your

ANGEL OF DARKNESS

realm Hades. I would not call that a coincidence."

The brothers all looked at each other and all agreed Anubis did have a point.

"But what can we do about it if this is the enemy we were shown?" Zeus asked the group, "We all saw that being destroying out realms and causing us pain and death."

"There may be a way to confront this being" Hades said.

"I think it would be wiser to try and understand it better before rushing into battle against this unknown being" Anubis suggested.

"So, you're saying we should just sit back and wait for this being to come for us?" Zeus asked.

"I'm saying that this being seems to be very strong and we know nothing about it." Anubis said.

"Well do you have any thoughts about what we can learn about this being from these two encounters other than that it is strong?" Poseidon asked the group.

"What if the reason it can escape our sight so easily is because we're looking for darkness in the wrong form?" Anubis suggested.

"What do you mean?" Zeus asked.

"I'm suggesting it may be here on Earth, in plain sight, in the form of a mortal." Anubis told them.

"A mortal?" Hades questioned.

"Yes, you said you searched for a being of pure darkness, but you searched for one shrouded by a shadowed form. Perhaps looking for a being in mortal form with immense power possibly emanating from it would be where we should look to try to identify where this being is. That will allow us to track its movements more efficiently." Anubis said.

"Power emanating from them, you mean similar to that of our children?" Poseidon questioned.

"Yes, similar to your children," Anubis said. "But I think other beings aside from demi-Gods, but still similar, should be considered here."

"Are you saying that we should observe our children and that they may be possible targets for this dark being to hide within?" Poseidon asked.

"I am not saying that" Anubis replied. "I am saying that similar to your children who emit some form of energy reflecting to the power which you've passed down onto them; this being of darkness may emit a similar energy."

"Why do you think that we should consider beings other than demi-Gods to be possible beings that we should observe?" Zeus asked.

"I don't believe demi-Gods could be bothered by this being" Anubis said.

"Why do you believe that?" Hades asked.

"Because the powers you've passed onto your children have awakened within them and are now protecting them from powers such as this." Ma'at said as she sat up.

"Ma'at are you sure you should be moving right now?" Anubis asked as he rushed to his partner.

"I'm fine," she replied, "I just need to sit up for a moment."

"Our powers have awakened within our children?" Poseidon asked as Ma'at looked towards him.

ANGEL OF DARKNESS

"Yes, for example, your children can be healed from injury when they come into contact with water. This could not happen until their power deemed them worthy and awakened within their souls." Ma'at explained.

"Should the power within our children begin to affect them when they are born? Also how do you know all of this?" Zeus asked.

"To answer your second question first, The Ancients have mentioned these instances to me before in the past." Ma'at replied.

"How have they done that?" Anubis asked.

"These items I carry with me. I told you the Ancients crafted these long ago. Well, these items have wills of their own. They have often shown me many events of the past upon their own will. I believe that the power within demi-Gods holds the same willpower to choose when the time is right to awaken from within."

"So, you're saying this being of darkness most likely won't target our children because our powers have deemed them worthy of their power and are now protecting them?" Zeus asked.

"Exactly," Ma'at replied.

"Anubis, your suggestion is we investigate all the mortals on Earth in search of those who have energy auras surrounding their bodies?" Hades asked turning everyone back to their main concern.

"I believe that would be a good place to start, but it will be difficult to search all humans on earth at once, even for us. So, I think we should try to narrow our surveillance to areas where darkness presents itself in some form. Such as areas where night falls more often than others or places where fear lingers across the lands." Anubis suggested.

"Why do you believe areas of fear would be good places to search?" Poseidon asked.

"Because you said this enemy emits an energy which causes fear" Anubis said towards Hades. "So, places where fear is elevated may be a good indication of this being's presence."

"That does make sense." Zeus said. "We can enlist the help from other Gods in Olympus to extend our search parameters."

"We will consult with Ra and see if the Egyptians will agree in assisting you in the search" Ma'at followed.

"That would definitely make the search easier" Hades agreed.

"We will contact you if Ra agrees to help in the search" Anubis said before raising his scepter and howling loudly as his body glowed. "The barriers surrounding this realm have been temporarily disabled, go now and may we find this being with haste."

"I will consult the powers of the items and see if they can indicate any knowledge of this being we all fear," Ma'at said as she took back the scales that Anubis was still holding.

"Thank you" the Greek Gods said in unison before disappearing in a flash of light as they flew back to Olympus.

Chapter Twelve

YUKO SLOWLY WALKED into the core of the school. Now that she knew the truth about Max, she knew she would begin to see her surroundings differently. She would start to understand why the other students feared her friend. They feared the unknown. Many of the theories that circulated Max were just that, theories, no one really knew what had occurred that day, aside from Max and now Yuko. Not knowing the truth is what made the other students so easily afraid. Yuko decided that morning she would try to help Max be a friend to the school and not a problem child. But to do that, Yuko knew she would need some help. She saw that help sitting at a table near the rear end of the core.

"Hey Megan. Alex." Yuko said.

"Hey Yuko" they said, motioning her to sit down.

"How are you two doing today?" Yuko asked as she sat down.

"Fine just tired of all the snow that's been falling recently." Megan said.

"I heard it was supposed to snow again on Saturday and they were predicting at least another five centimeters." Alex said.

"Great that's going to be fun shoveling that out of the driveway." Megan said looking annoyed.

"You don't like having to shovel snow?" Yuko asked.

"Not when we get a mountain to try and move." Megan replied. "Seriously try it, it's more difficult than you think."

"I have a snow blower at my house, so as long as I go slowly with it, clearing large amounts of snow is not a problem." Alex bragged.

"Try doing it with your back at the wrong end of a shovel," Megan shot back.

They both stared at each other for a minute before Yuko interrupted them with some slight laughter.

"What's so funny?" Megan asked.

"The fact you two are fighting over something like that. I find it hilarious because of how you are arguing about it." Yuko said through hard breaths.

"I guess it is kind of funny how we are simply arguing about how we handle the large amounts of snow that we get here." Alex said.

Megan simply laughed under her breath in response.

ANGEL OF DARKNESS

"So, listen, can I ask you two something important?" Yuko said.

"What is it?" Megan asked.

"It's about Max, see I need your help with something I learned about her." Yuko said.

"What is it this time?" Alex asked.

"I'll tell you, but you have to promise not to tell anyone about this." Yuko said.

"We promise" Megan and Alex said in unison after a moment of glancing at each other.

"Ok well..." Yuko continued to tell them about the truth about what Max had experienced in her youth. Megan and Alex remained quiet throughout the story, but their faces showed great shock when Yuko finished her tale.

"I never knew it was that severe." Megan said with her eyes wide open.

"I heard she just got into trouble with the police, but I never expected that was the reason." Alex quickly followed.

"Yeah, it was hard for her to tell me, I'm not entirely sure as to why she even told me." Yuko said to their stunned faces.

"So, what do you need us for?" Megan asked.

"I need you to be there for her. She seems to be in a state of complete depression and loneliness, and I think she needs friends now more than anything. Only problem is that no one wants to try and be her friend because they fear her due of these rumors that have spread around the school." Yuko said.

"Well, you can count me in." Megan said quickly. "Max

has always seemed like a good person at heart."

"I'm in as well, Max has helped me through some tough times in school through the past year and I want to try and repay the favor now that I know why she was always suffering on the inside. How are we going to help her?" Alex followed.

"That's just it; I'm not sure as to how we can help her. I was hoping you guys might have some ideas." Yuko said softly.

"Maybe we could just offer her a friend." Megan suggested. "It seems like she needs one at the moment."

"That's what we've been trying to do recently. But how can we show her that in a way where she accepts us?"

"Maybe just with a smile and helping hand?" Alex suggested, "friendships aren't just about words you know."

Yuko thought about that for a moment. Alex did have a point. "Ok, let's try that."

"Ok but it might be best to try and talk to her at the same time?" Megan said.

"I agree" Alex said, "so when to you want to talk to her about this?"

"How about after school at the White Peak restaurant down in the shopping district? I've looked into it and that place is empty in the afternoon until around 5, so we can get some privacy there,"

"Sounds good, we'll meet you there after school, but don't tell Max why you're leading here there. I think it will be better if she doesn't know we are there until she arrives."

"Alright I think I can manage that. Thanks, you guys and

ANGEL OF DARKNESS

remember this stays between us."

"No problem" Alex said.

"We can keep a secret" Megan assured as the bell rang and each girl went off to her respective class.

The rest of the day went smoothly. Max and Yuko continued to move through the crowds. Yuko finally understood why they were afraid. If rumors of the police being involved in some way for a person's past it would make sense for others around that person to be concerned. This environment however was surrounded by fear and not much concern.

Megan and Alex did meet the two of them for lunch as they usually did, and just as the promised, they kept quiet about their newfound knowledge. Yuko kept an eye out for what she could use as a distraction for several minutes while Megan and Alex got a head start for their plan after school. At the end of the last class, she found the opportunity.

"Hey Max check this out."

"What is it?"

They stared at a poster about the upcoming school hockey tournament.

"You like hockey Yuko?"

"It is interesting to watch. I saw a game the other day on TV, and it was exciting. Do people usually get into fights when they play?"

"Sometimes they do. The players get knocked around into the boards a lot and sometimes the players want to take it a step further when they've had enough. That's when the gloves come off and they start swinging at each other. It doesn't happen often, but when it does it can be pretty entertaining."

"Why is it entertaining?" Yuko asked "I found it overextending the game's already tough nature."

"That's what makes it interesting. When two players put their skills to the test in ways other than their puck handling and speed when rushing down the ice." Max explained. "Are you thinking of joining the school's team?"

"No way, I can't skate."

"Maybe I can teach you sometime?"

"Would you do that?"

"Winter is settling in, and the town is going to shift into the ski and skate thrilled state. I think it would be fun, because it wouldn't be any fun if everyone else is having a good time and you're sitting there on the sidelines. Can you ski or skate at all?"

"I have never tried to ski before. I have tired skating, but I could never get my balance down correctly." That was true. In Japan when she was younger, she wanted to join the national ice-skating team. Seeing the skaters turn ice into a dancefloor fascinated Yuko, but whenever she tried to skate, she just could not stay up. The blades were just so thin, and Yuko could never figure out how to balance herself against the ice. Her mother could skate like a pro. She always turned the ice rink into a stage and gracefully moved like snow being whisked by the wind over a mountain peak.

Her father on the other hand couldn't skate at all, Yuko guessed that was where her skill from; or rather lack of

ANGEL OF DARKNESS

skill. They had tried to help Yuko get a handle on her balance, but for some reason she never could get it down. That was five years ago.

"Come on Yuko, it will be fun, I'll even help you with getting into the flow of skating." Max suggested suddenly. Yuko looked over at Max. Her expression hadn't changed since she brought up the talk about winter sports and getting on the ice. She clearly had some experience, a lot more than Yuko did, so maybe she could teach Yuko a thing or two.

"Okay, let's do it." Yuko said, "But I don't have a pair of skates, I dropped them and never bothered to pick them up after I lost my interest." That was partially true, the truth was that she grew out of them and never bothered to tell her parents that they didn't fit anymore. So, she left them in Japan with one of her neighbors whose daughter wanted to learn how to ice skate.

"I've got a pair of skates that might fit you. If they don't then we can just head down to the skate shop and pick up a pair."

"Thanks Max, but I think it would be better if I just got my own pair that way I know they will work for me."

As the two walked out into the cold Yuko remembered the plan she'd set up earlier that day.

"Hey Max, I just remembered, I'm meeting Megan and Alex for a while to get an afterschool snack downtown. Want to come?" Yuko quickly realized that there was some slight desperation in her voice, hopefully Max didn't notice. She tried to look innocent as Max turned to look at her.

"Sure, I didn't have anything planned after school

anyway." Max said. Yuko sighed under her breath; so far the plan was working.

"The two headed down the roads through the downtown district for a while. Yuko explained that Megan and Alex had gone on ahead because they knew of a good place and wanted to go ahead of her to get seats. "They didn't tell me where it would be though" Yuko said.

"I guess they really like surprises then," Max said.

They kept walking along the roads until Yuko heard someone calling her name. Looking around she saw Megan coming towards her and Max.

"Hey Yuko" she said before noticing Max "hey Max how you doing?"

"I'm fine, how are you?"

"Good."

"Where's Alex?" Yuko asked.

"She's getting a table over at White Peak, that's where we decided to go as they have deals on their chicken wings today. You okay with that?" Alex replied.

"Sure, sounds good." Yuko replied. "That alright with you Max?"

"Yeah sure, I could use some good hot wings right now with this cold wind."

The three headed down the opposite direction from where Yuko and Max were initially heading over to the restaurant. When they arrived, they were greeted by a nice man who took them inside and showed them the table where Alex was already sitting.

"Hey girls," Alex said as the other three sat down.

ANGEL OF DARKNESS

"Hey Alex," Max and Yuko replied.

"How's your day been going?" Alex asked towards Max.

"Good, I finally got the drawers for my bookshelf finished in construction class, so now I can move onto my next project once the teacher grades it."

"What are you making next?" Yuko asked.

"I decided to go with a table with a rounded base" Max replied.

Their waiter came by as Max finished talking; he asked if the girls wanted anything to drink. They decided to just get water to start.

"So, you're making a table?" Megan asked trying to continue the conversation.

"Yeah. What about you Yuko you're almost done your four-legged table right?"

"I actually finished it, just waiting for the teacher to grade it." Yuko replied, "after that I think I might make a cabinet or something."

"Cool" Alex said. "I wish I could have joined that class."

"You weren't able to?" Max asked.

"No, I couldn't fit it into my schedule. My options came down to one available slot in my timetable and I had to decide between construction or forensics sciences. I decided to go with the forensics class because I thought it would be more interesting."

"That's too bad." Yuko said. "I guess I'll have to figure out what I would like to do for my options next year."

"Don't fill up with option classes though." Megan told

her "I did that at first and they told me I had to change my schedule because I filled my timetable with options and avoided the second-year programs I was required to take."

"I remember that." Alex laughed "you were upset for weeks."

"I hate social studies, so I did not want to take it if possible. But I didn't have a choice considering I apparently need to take it to graduate." Megan replied. Max, Yuko, and Alex all laughed. Megan picked up one of the menus and apparently that was the end of that embarrassing moment.

Their waiter came back with their water and asked if they were ready to order anything. Everyone quickly skimmed the menu and decided to split two plates of wings, one of salt and pepper, the other of hot sauce.

After the man left Max continued the conversation "so have you been enjoying your time here so far Yuko?"

"Yeah, it's been awesome. You guys have been really amazing friends." Yuko replied.

"You're pretty interesting yourself." Alex said, "I don't know what it is, but you just seem to connect to those around you."

"That sounds like you have some feelings for her" Megan taunted.

"No, I don't!! I meant there is something different about Yuko that I've never noticed with many of the other people who live in this town. I've lived here my whole life, so I know what I'm talking about." Alex blurted out before Megan could continue with her smug look. Yuko and Max both giggled at Megan's attempt to turn this into something beyond a casual get together with friends.

ANGEL OF DARKNESS

Yuko decided it was about time to break the ice since they had time before their order would be ready and they were all in a good mood. Looking towards Megan and Alex she nodded slightly, and they both nodded back to indicate that they agreed it seemed like a good time to tell Max that they had planned this whole scenario.

"Hey Max, this is kind of difficult for me to say but I feel like now is the best time to say it" Yuko said as Max turned in response.

"What is it?"

"Well... to be honest the three of us, Megan, Alex and I planned out this little event earlier today. For a reason beyond simply getting together with friends"

"What do you mean?" Max asked.

"I... um.... I told Megan and Alex the truth about what happened to you when you were younger."

Max's face instantly turned to sudden fear. "What?... Why would you do that?" She asked frantically jumping out of her chair.

"Because she needed our help" Megan told her.

"Your help?"

"Yes" Alex added joining the conversation. "She's concerned for you and feels that you are blaming yourself entirely for what you did. Yuko told us because she knew Megan and I are trying to help you. We want you to know that you aren't alone in facing this fact. Before Yuko told us, we were both following everyone else at school in the multitude of rumors."

"No one was entirely positive about what happened to

you." Megan stated. "It was scary because you were always a nice person and several years ago when you... well did what you did... you changed dramatically. No one knew the entire truth, hell we don't even know where the stories originated. But we wanted you to know that because we know the truth, we still accept you for who you are."

Max stared at them, her face covered in fear, she couldn't bring herself to believe what was happening. She felt betrayed by Yuko due to the fact that she had revealed her greatest secret to two people who she never really had any communication with.

"You accept the horrible reality about what happened to me?" Max asked towards the two who were trying to comfort her.

"It's hard to come to grips with it, but I feel that we now have a clear view as to what happened to you. Before we had no idea it was so severe, but now we know the truth and we agree it has shed some enlightenment on why you were so distant from everyone in the school and why you are always paranoid by those around you." Megan stated not breaking eye contact with Max.

"I feel the same." Alex told her. "I'll admit I feared you because I didn't know the truth about what had happened. The stories that I heard only contained information that pointed towards you and the police being involved in something. But other than that, I didn't know anything."

Max didn't move. She just stared at the three girls who all stared back at her. She didn't know what to do. *Does she run in fear of being betrayed? Does she stay, deny her own past, and try to move on without her past by using these three as scapegoats for her fear?*

ANGEL OF DARKNESS

No, I can't do that. I've ran and tried to hide from my own path. I can't do that again, but I don't know what to do about these people who now know what happened.

Max slowly sat back down and looked over each of the girls in front of her. No one spoke then Max asked, "and what do you think now that you know the truth?" She asked as she hung her head slightly but keeping eye contact.

Megan was the first to speak "it's scary, I'm not going to deny that, but at the same time it's helpful."

"Helpful?" Max said.

"Because now we're not shrouded in the mystery of why you always ran away and why you always got scared whenever anyone said anything about what you did." Alex followed.

"And why does that help you?" Max said.

"Because now that we know the reason behind your fear, we can figure out a way of how to help you cope with it." Yuko said.

"You seem to be staying closed off within yourself; I noticed that began after the rumors started to spread" Alex said. "That was a year and a half ago. You've kept yourself locked within the past and it seems like you've never tried to move on."

"You think I haven't?" Max asked. "You think I haven't tried to forget? Everywhere I go I feel like someone knows about what I did; either from having figured it out themselves or just following along with those rumors. I've been alone for almost two years now and I can't ignore the emotions. The trauma I felt when I did what I did. I've tried but it won't go away no matter what I do."

"I know I said this the other day when you told me the truth," Yuko said after a minute where no one spoke. "But perhaps you can't let it go because it's changed you in a way where it's not you who has to adapt but those around you."

"That's exactly what I was thinking." Megan said. "We've talked it over and Alex and I are willing to adapt and accept the new you."

"I agree with that with no objections." Alex followed.

Max looked over the girls sitting across from her again. Maybe they could help her deal with these emotions she could not rid herself of. Max felt something rush down her spine, causing her to shiver, and she felt like she maybe could trust these girls with the truth. It seemed like they all felt the same way and Max did feel accepted within the little group that they had between the four of them.

"Sounds like you've found yourself a good group of friends." A voice said beside the table. The girls turned their heads and saw a middle-aged man who looked like he was in his forties; he wore a black sweater, blue jeans and was sitting in a wheelchair. The man was looking at Max and she was staring back at him.

"You know him Max?" Yuko asked noticing Max's suddenly calm, but still scared, face.

Max looked back at Yuko "Yeah, he's my father."

"You're her..." Yuko began to say towards the man before Max cut her off.

"What are you doing here Dad?"

"To answer your question," he said turning to Yuko "yes,

ANGEL OF DARKNESS

I'm her father, name's Jim, it's nice to meet you. To answer your question Max, my friends asked me if I wanted to grab some beer with them and watch the Edmonton Oilers play the opening game of the season." Jim tilted the blue hat he was wearing which held the Oilers team symbol.

"The hockey seasons started already?" Megan asked.

"Yup, the puck drops in about half an hour. I came here with Ted to get some drinks before the game. Bob and Joe are coming later after they finish work." Jim said. "So, Max I overheard your little conversation a minute ago and it sounds like these friends of yours are very open minded and willing to help you."

"You don't even know what they want to help me out with," Max said.

"You're talking about the event that occurred several years ago with that robber who came into our house." Jim said to Max's stunned face. "I can see the fear in your eyes that's been with you ever since that day" he looked down as if contemplating his thoughts.

"Is it true?" Alex asked, "what happened?"

Jim didn't say anything he just glanced towards Max who looked away, after about a minute she nodded without looking up.

"Yes... it is true." Jim said after receiving the silent confirmation to proceed. "We were victims of an attempted robbery, and my daughter was forced to make a choice no child should ever be faced with."

The whole table was silent. Megan and Alex constantly glanced at each other, Yuko kept looking between Max and her father; trying to figure out what to say, Max just looked down and didn't make eye contact with anyone. Jim kept his eyes on Max, glancing towards Yuko, Megan, and Alex from time to time. Their food arrived and Jim quietly asked the waiter to silently put the food on the nearby table. The man complied and backed off trying not to break the silence.

"Not a day goes by where I don't blame myself for what happened." Jim said after another minute.

"Why do you blame yourself?" Alex asked.

"Because I was a soldier during the Second World War." Jim said "I should have been able to fight that intruder off, but he got the jump on me and that was enough for him to paralyze my legs for life. Don't get me wrong I can live without the use of my legs, but the pain of what happened afterwards with my daughter, was just too strong to rid easily."

"I still can't forget the face of that man." Max said. "The face that he had right before he died. Complete anger and satisfaction at the same time. As if he was happy with the deed I had done."

"Why would he have been happy?" Yuko asked.

"I don't know." Max replied, "but I do know I can't forget that look he gave me no matter how hard I try."

"I can only imagine what you must have felt like when it happened." Alex said, "it must have been awful."

"It was. And it still is."

"Well, you don't have to face this alone." Megan said, "we're here for you when you need us."

"Exactly, that's all in the past, why don't we all begin a

ANGEL OF DARKNESS

new journey together?" Alex said.

Max looked up and glanced over the faces of the people sitting around her. Yuko, Megan, and Alex all wore facial gestures filled with kindness and friendship. Their expressions almost illuminated the area; Max could even swear that Yuko was glowing for an odd reason. But there was also a window behind her so that could have been why that was. Maybe they could help her deal with her problem. They all were accepting of what she had done and were willing to be there for her when she needed it. She certainly felt like she needed them now. Before she knew it the feelings around the area overwhelmed her and she began crying.

"Max?" Alex asked quietly over Max's silent tears. Max quickly realized what she was doing, but she couldn't stop herself.

"I'm fine" She said, "just happy."

"Happy?" Yuko asked.

"I've never really had anyone try and understand the hardships I went through. You guys are the first to even try." Max explained while wiping her face.

"Well actually to be honest it was Yuko who was the first to try and help you." Alex said, "She was the first one who you told the truth too; Megan and I just followed with the rumors that circulated and took them as a mixed up puzzle that would never be completed."

"That may be true, but this experience has helped me realize that there are some people around me who I can trust and who accept me regardless of my past."

"Well out past is what shapes the story of our future."

Megan said. "So maybe your past, however dark it may be, has changed you into someone new. That is who we see today, and this person is a good friend."

"I feel the same way" Yuko said.

"Same here, no objections" Alex followed "This chapter's over, let's start a new one."

"Well Max" Jim said, "Think you can give your friend a chance?"

Max glanced around once more; her eyes still wet from her tears. Everyone was smiling at her, she felt like new. The face of the robber began fading from her mind. Replaced by the faces of those staring at her.

"I don't have to give them a try." Max said smiling back at everyone "I already trust them."

"That's good to hear." Jim said, "Now if you'll excuse me ladies, I have to get back to my friends as the game is about to start."

The girls said goodbye as Jim spun around and sped off to his friends. Two of whom arrived at a neighboring table while Jim was talking with the girls. He asked the waiter to move the girl's food over to their table as he moved by.

"Go ahead Max, you take the first one." Megan said as their food was set down on their table.

"Don't mind if I do Megan," Max said. She did feel like this was the start of a new adventure. No more being alone, afraid, always looked at with fear. She would have her friends by her side now and, although their group was small, it was enough for her.

Chapter Thirteen

THE WEATHER THE next day brought a cold front, and with it a mountain of snow and cold wind that ripped the skin from flesh. Yuko learned about these harsh conditions the hard way as she raced back home from the bus stop. She and her mother had to run to the appliance store to get a new coil of wire as her father wanted to re-wire some of the old outlets in the house. A few of the wires that were installed when the house was built were now worn down and the wiring within was exposed. Thankfully, Yuko's father had some electrical skills and knew he could fix the problem.

It felt like heaven to feel the rush of warm air as they entered the house. Yuko quickly took off her jacket and let her body release the trapped heat from her body. Cool air instantly rushed over her body, sweat poured from her body as she adjusted to the change in temperature.

"Well... that was fun." Her mother said.

"If you count being torn apart by wind fun then yes it was a blast."

"Her mother laughed. "Can you take these to your father?" She asked as she handed Yuko the wires and took her coat off.

"Sure thing" Yuko replied taking off her boots. She went downstairs where the fuse box was and found her father working on the floor near it. Several tools were surrounding him, and he was currently unscrewing an outlet in the corner of the room.

"Hey Dad" Yuko said from a safe distance.

"Hey Yuko" her father said turning around. "It's ok you can come over; I turned off the power to this area so there isn't any electricity running through these wires."

"Here's the wiring you needed," Yuko said handing him the package.

"Thanks sweetie, want me to show you how to do this?"

"Sure."

Yuko sat and listened as her father explained how to remove the outlet and expose the wiring behind it. The outlet had a connecting end, which completed the electric circuit and powered what was connected to the wiring system. The wires that were behind the outlet were worn down and had too much of the wires exposed behind it. Her father showed her how she had to cut the wires;

ANGEL OF DARKNESS

making sure a measure of wiring remained exposed so they could connect the new wires together. Once that was done, they grabbed the new wire and cut it to length. Grabbing a knife her father demonstrated how to strip the cover and expose the wiring within. Then using electrical tape, connect the old wires to the new one and then to the outlet. Once that was all secure it was a simple matter of screwing the outlet back into the wall.

"That's all there is too it." Her father explained as Yuko screwed the last screw into the wall.

"That was really easy." She was surprised at how simple the task was.

"Well, that was a simple fix. Some of the wiring around the house needs some more work, more than what I might be able to do. I'll look at it and if I can't fix it, I'll call an electrician."

Yuko and her father packed up the tools and headed upstairs where Yuko's mother was in the kitchen warming up some tea. The three sat down at the table while the blizzard ragged outside; snow blew furiously across the window.

"So, Yuko how has school been going?" Her father asked after a while.

"It's okay."

"How's your friend been? You seemed really concerned about her these last few days." Her mother asked.

"Actually, she's a lot better than she was."

"Why is that?"

Yuko thought about how to answer that question. *Would*

it be wrong to get her family involved in Max's past? No, she shouldn't get them worried about that event. That was between Max and her family. Yuko saw how Max had been under pressure letting her feelings go the other day with her, Megan, and Alex. "She recently let go of something that had been emotionally attached to her for a long time." Yuko said after a minute. "So, she seems like she is a lot happier now."

"That's good to hear," Yuko's mother said.

"Do you know what it was that caused her that distress?" Her father asked.

Yuko hoped they wouldn't ask that question. "Yes, I do, she told me, and I promised I would keep it to myself. Two of my other friends were with us and they both agreed as well to keep it a secret. We would let Max decide to let others know about it."

Both her parents stayed quiet as she explained that. "Well, that's very good if you to care about your friend and to respect her wishes to keep whatever happened to her a secret." Her father said.

"It was kind of odd though. I felt something strange happen before I asked her about the event myself." Yuko said before she had a chance to stop herself; unsure if that was the right thing to say.

"What do you mean?" Her mother asked.

"It was like I could feel the wind talk to me after I asked her. It told me that if I wanted the answer to my question, that was the right moment to ask."

Yuko looked up and saw both her parents were staring at her. Their eyes were wide, and they looked worried.

"What?" Yuko asked.

ANGEL OF DARKNESS

"You heard the wind talk to you?" Her mother asked, glancing over to her husband who glanced back.

"I'm not sure what it was, but I definitely felt something." Yuko said. "It was like the town was telling me to keep going with my mission to find the truth and help me friend." Yuko looked up to see both her parents looking at her as if she was in her own world at the moment. It was odd. "Are you guys ok?"

"Um... yeah we're fine. Just thinking." Her mother quickly said.

"Thinking about what?"

"Nothing, I just some odd thoughts about what you just said. About hearing the wind talking to you." Her father said.

"Oh. That was just an odd feeling. It doesn't mean anything." Yuko replied. But she sensed that her parents weren't being honest with her. They had reacted strangely to her story, and it was as if they weren't telling her something. In fact, she was sure of it. There was something off about her parents. They never acted this way before. It was like they were scared. They kept glancing over her as if she were a stranger.

"I get the feeling you're not telling me something." Yuko said.

"Why do you think that?" Her mother asked.

"You're acting kind of weird, almost like what I said before was something crazy and unnatural."

"Well, it's just that... don't you think your imagining things when you said the wind talked to you?" Yuko's father asked.

"Like I said before it was just a feeling." Yuko said, "it most likely doesn't mean anything."

"I guess that solves the problem before it starts." Her mother said.

"I guess so" Yuko said. Thought she said that she didn't believe it, she knew they were hiding something. "I'm going to take a nap."

"Feeling a bit tired?" Her mother asked.

"Yeah, kind of," Yuko replied.

"Okay, go get some rest" her father said.

Yuko got up and headed to her room. As she reached the halfway point of the stairs, she felt something within her begin to stir. She had the sense something was trying to call her. Looking back at her parents she saw that they were looking at each other and holding hands on the table. Both were quiet and didn't say anything. Seeing her parents together like that, happy; together, it seemed to open some sort of feeling within her. She thought it was loneliness, except she wasn't alone. She had Max, Alex, and Megan. Whatever that feeling was Yuko decided to let it go and just go take her nap. She was tired even thought it was the middle of the day.

Yuko got to her room and glanced out the window. The blizzard still raged outside; the snowflakes were so thick you could catch them easily with your tongue. She wasn't a kid anymore, but those memories of messing around in the snow with her friends were still in her memories. Staring through the window Yuko thought she saw something black fly through the white cover. A blink later and it was gone. Maybe she was more tired than she thought. Jumping onto her bed Yuko closed her eyes and gradually let the sound of the wind outside put her to sleep.

The black eagle flew through the snowy mist. Yellow eyes scanning the area as its large wings sliced through the air. Flying with the wind as it was carried higher above the ground, the eagle's eyes became fixed on the peak of the mountain which it scaled. Breaking the mist and emerging within the glow of the sun the eagle turned and glided towards the peak where another eagle stood. This eagle only bared its head and sharp talons, in place of wings the eagle had arms and legs connected to a strong human body. A large scepter lay across the creature's chest as its gold eyes met the yellow glow of the black eagle which circled overhead. Taking a step back the eagled man watched the black eagle land upon the rocks. A bright flash later and the eagle was replaced with a white bearded man with strong muscles, a bolt of lightning clutched tightly in his fist. Both beings took turns exchanging bows of respect towards the other. Then the eagled man spoke.

"Have a good flight Zeus, King of Olympus?"

"It would have been better if I wasn't forced to use a method of cover to investigate the area great Ra King of the Sun."

"Yes, well with the news Anubis informed me of I thought it was a wise choice. Can't risk you being spotted by this dark shadow Hades encountered."

"So, you accept that my brothers and I were correct? There is a shadow out there threatening the balance which we worked so hard to achieve."

"After what occurred I have no doubts something has awoken. The Scales of Balance have never been altered in such a way before, so that leads me to accept there is no more cause for suspicion against what you were shown by The Ancients."

"I'm glad to hear you have finally come to see The Ancients were correct."

"Yes, well the matter still stands that we do not know this being's whereabouts or what it even hopes to achieve."

"I've flown across the northern lands and found nothing. No hints or clues towards this being's presence."

"What about your brothers and that speedster you have with you?"

"Hades is contemplating what that shadow wanted within the Underworld, Poseidon has his closest and most trusted merfolk searching the seas, those who are semi-mers are also searching the coastal towns. Hermes is relaying messages between the Olympians who are assisting my brothers and me in our search for answers."

"Well if I may offer you the support of the Egyptian Gods in the search for this dark being, I believe that may be able to increase the speed at which we locate this being."

"You're offering to help us in our search?"

"I am."

"Thank you for…"

"However," Ra interrupted "We will only help you locate this being, we cannot engage in any form of conflict with this creature should it be hostile towards us Gods."

"You will not help us fight this being! Why?"

"I have to think about my own people's safety. The Ancients showed this enemy to you. This is your fight. I will not risk the lives of my own followers in such a task. One of my followers, Ma'at, has already collapsed and lost a great amount of strength. I take that as a warning not to become involved in this fated encounter of yours."

"A warning that she could not avoid thanks to those ancient scales draining her power in response to the presence of something dark passing through her realm. Your territory. This concerns both our groups of deities now."

Ra stared back at Zeus as he listened to those words. His golden eyes clashed with Zeus' clear blue.

"My mind is made up Zeus." Ra spoke without breaking eye contact. "I will help you find this foe of yours, but I cannot engage this being should it cost the life of one of my followers. I am a just ruler, but I must protect my own."

Zeus was furious as Ra's unwillingness to help him and his followers in conflict should this shadow become the threat Zeus feared it to be. Zeus kept a still face and did not let his anger show. Without the Egyptian's help it could take much longer to locate this enemy; and Zeus guessed that was time they could not afford to lose.

"I understand. I too have to keep my followers and brothers' safety in mind. I thank you for the assistance and will accept your offer in helping us search for this being." Zeus said.

"Let us just hope we find this being quickly before anyone else has to suffer. I trust that Hermes can handle being the messenger for the Egyptians in addition to the Greeks?" Ra spoke.

"He can handle it; I trust him like I trust my own

brothers."

"That is good to hear. I will contact my followers and tell them what we will search for. Anubis and Ma'at will remain in the depths of the tombs as Ma'at is still weak and I trust Anubis to protect her with my life." With that Ra disappeared in a flash of light leaving Zeus alone atop the mountain.

"Let's hope you change your ways when the time for combat arrives." Zeus said before spreading his arms and changing back into his eagle form to complete his patrol route.

Several hours passed before Zeus decided to head home to get some rest. His wings dragged behind him and he began to feel like weights had been to them. Summoning lightning from the sky Zeus teleported himself back to Olympus, emerging from his eagle form in the process. After stretching his tired arms Zeus headed into the main chamber. Upon entering he was met by Hades and Hermes.

"Hello brother" Hades said as Zeus walked in "How was your meeting with Ra?"

"He has agreed to help us with the search for this dark being, but he won't have the Egyptians enter combat should this enemy rise up against us." Zeus replied taking a seat.

"He won't help us fight this foe?" Hades asked.

"I asked him those exact words. He said that he had to remain cautious about the safety of his fellow Gods. He doesn't want to risk their lives against a being that can disrupt those Scales of Balance as greatly as this being did."

"You feel the same way about us, right?" Hermes asked.

"Of course, I do, I care for the safety of all of my fellow

deities. I just feel like if we do find this foe, we will need support should it engage us." Zeus replied.

"Ra will come around," Hades said. "He will once he knows what kind of foe we face. We will also learn more once we find this enemy."

"Yes, once we find this enemy. Only problem is that I searched everywhere around these northern areas of the world and only found a few small areas where fear and darkness loomed over the lands." Zeus said. "Did you find anything new about why this being entered the Underworld Hades?"

"No," Hades replied "There was nothing disrupted within my realm. Even my castle was undisturbed as the barrier surrounding it was active and untampered."

"Then what was the point of that being entering the Underworld?" Hermes asked. "I've been there many times myself and it seems like there is nothing worth taking back from that pit of agony."

"You have not been there recently since you can no longer enter the realm freely," Hades said.

"Yeah thanks to you wanting extra privacy with that gate of yours," Hermes replied.

"I've told you that Chiron and Cerberus will let you through if you just talk to them," Hades explained.

"You should put that dog on a leash; all he does is shoot fire at those who come by the gate." Hermes said. "Anyway, that's not the issue right now. Zeus you said you encountered several areas in the mortal realm which had essence of fear?"

"Yes, however none of the areas were strong enough that

MICHAEL MCGEE

I would be concerned." Zeus said. "Actually… there was one area within a small mountain town with a rather large aura surrounding it."

"People in those towns are probably worried about forest fires burning down their precious landscape," Hades said.

"I don't think that was the case," Zeus explained. "Many of the mortals living there, they seemed to be afraid of something, however I couldn't tell what that was."

Several minutes passed where no one spoke. Hades began thinking about what could have possibly been the reason for the shadow entering his realm. Something did not feel right, there had to be something that he missed.

"I think we may need to take a closer look at that mountain town." Zeus suggested.

"How do you suggest we do that?" Hades asked. "If Anubis is right and that shadow hides in areas containing fear and darkness, we may run right into it. If that area turns out to be a trap, we are unprepared for."

"Why not send scouts ahead to observe the area?" Hermes said. "You could send some creatures under your control, which the shadow might not target if it detects them, and they could search the area for anything or anyone that may relate to this being."

Hades and Zeus both turned to Hermes who took a cautious step back. He didn't like the glare he was receiving. The brothers turned to each other for a moment before turning back.

"That actually sounds like a good idea," Hades said.

"We could communicate freely from our realms, and no

one would know about it," Zeus added.

"But we'll have to have them take human form in order for them to blend in," Hades stated.

"That's not a problem, if needed the creatures can easily shed that fragile shell and retreat or engage if necessary." Zeus said. "Hermes you may want to take a step back for this."

Hermes complied and retreated a few steps as Zeus and Hades both raised their arms. Four pillars rose from the ground; two of marble which spawned a white portal between them, and two of darkness which spawned a portal of fire between them.

"Come" Hades and Zeus called together.

The portals glowed as the creatures emerged. From the white portal came an eagle with four legs and bright white wings, a griffin, which bowed low to its master. From the portal of fire emerged a fox, bright yellow with orange flames dancing along its body. The fox too bowed low to its leader Hades. After a moment, the creatures rose in unison.

"We want you to go to the mortal world and search for beings among them who emit strong levels of energy," Hades told the creatures.

"Those you find are to be reported to us for examinations" Zeus followed "Under no account are you to harm anyone without our express orders."

"Most importantly if you encounter a being bathed in darkness you must not engage it. We only want you to find those who emit anything that is unnatural to the human realm."

The creatures bowed in acknowledgment before

bursting into light and flame which teleported them to the world below.

"Let us hope they do not encounter this dark being" Zeus said.

"That's all we can do at this point is hope." Hades agreed "I'm going to go back to the Underworld; I need to have a closer look around there as something still doesn't seem right regarding that shadows entry into my realm."

Before going, Hades gave Zeus a purple crystal saying "use this if you need to contact me, it's easier than trying to enter my realm as my gate will remain closed. Simply call me and it will open a portal to a similar black crystal I have with me. Chiron and I use these to communicate when he has someone alive that wants entry into the Underworld." With that Hades disappeared in a blast of dark and purple shadows.

"I hope this ends well for all of us." Hermes said as Zeus took a seat.

"Let us hope." Zeus said once again.

Chapter Fourteen

SNOW COVERED THE ground upon which Yuko ran, her shoes making deep impressions in the ground. Dashing through the trees she began to think why she was running. She didn't know why she even began; all she knew was she had to escape what was pursuing her. Looking back however her gaze was met with fire which singed the ground around the flames. Turned the trees to ashes in seconds.

Yuko tried to remember why this was happening to her as she ran on. Before she could process any thoughts, she heard a loud growl behind her. Turning back, she saw a creature running through the flames, a fox bathed in the glow of the fire. The flames danced as the fox pursued its target. Rushing forward the fox dashed before her cutting off her path. Yuko was forced to stop before the flames; turning around she saw the fox had also stopped. They stared at each other as the head rose around them.

"My master wants to meet you" the fox spoke towards the terrified face of its captive.

"And... Who is that?" Yuko somehow managed to say in her paranoid state.

"The ruler of death, Hades" the fox snarled back.

Yuko didn't say anything, she only stared. *Ruler of the dead? Am I about to die?*

"Enough stalling, time is of the essence, my master wants you dead." The fox said followed by a loud growl. The flames quickly converged around the area as the fox pounced. Yuko's body began burning as the flames engulfed her body; the fox's teeth grabbed her arm and pierce her bone. Yuko screamed as she was tossed to the ground. The fox lay a paw on top of her chest, trapping her against the heat. Looking around Yuko thought she saw a figure watching them from the trees, the image was quickly lost to the flames as Yuko turned back to face the fox. Closing her eyes, she screamed in terror as the light from the fire burned through her eyelids.

Her screams rang in her ears as she jumped up from her bed. Breathing heavily, she tried to focus, tried to at least, but her body was heavy, and her chest ached. She quickly felt around her body, nothing seemed broken, just covered in sweat. Lying back down she tried to understand why these dreams kept occurring.

What was the reason behind the forest, the fox, the

ANGEL OF DARKNESS

flames, and the surrounding darkness? Why did she always wake up in pain? So many questions with no answers. She needed to talk to someone; her parents would think she was crazy again so she wouldn't bother asking them. There was only one person who might be able to help her; one person who may have some sort of answer thanks to past experiences dealing with pain and suffering. Yuko got up, grabbed her coat, and headed off towards Max's house.

"Why do you think I would be able to help you out with that kind of problem?" Max asked after Yuko told her about the consecutive dreams and about how she felt pain after they ended.

"Because I thought you may have experienced similar effects after you well… Did what you did." Yuko said, she still wasn't able to say Max killed someone without feeling sorry for her. So much so that she couldn't say anything linking back to that event without pausing.

"That was more psychological than physical" Max said, "It was the memories that stayed with me."

Yuko looked out across the field from the bench that they were sitting on. The snow had stopped shortly after she had woken up. She'd spotted Max in a field as she walked to her house.

"You had a similar dream in class the other day, right?" Max asked.

"Yeah, I did, only that one was different, there was no fire involved, how did you know about it?"

"I heard you fell asleep and woke up screaming. Word travels fast at school."

"Do you think it means anything?"

"What, your dreams?" Max asked. Yuko nodded. "I don't know what to think. The fox in this latest one, you said that it spoke to you?"

"Yeah it did," Yuko said as a chill ran down her spine. "It said that Hades wanted to meet me."

"Hades? The Greek God of Death?"

"I guess; I don't really know much about those Gods. I've heard some of the myths and legends about them, but I stick to the Gods of my own religion for belief."

"Do you have any reason to be thinking about the Greek God of the Dead at all?"

"No, I don't, and that's what is confusing me."

"It's confusing to me too, so much so that I don't know if I can help you with this problem." Max said as she rose "I'm sorry but I have to be getting back now; I hope you can figure out what the cause of these problems are."

"Thanks, but I feel like that is going to be harder than I think."

Max left and Yuko decided to walk for a bit, she felt dizzy and needed to stretch her legs to warm them up. She glanced around as she walked through the neighborhood. Several people were shoveling snow with their families, an elderly man was sitting on a porch swing smoking a pipe, and two men were leaning up against a tree talking to each other.

Just another normal day Yuko thought as she walked along the road *as normal as it gets around here for these people I guess.*

The two men under the tree leaned against it loosely,

ANGEL OF DARKNESS

keeping their bodies primed in case they had to move. They talked back and forth in a low voice, talking about the people they were observing.

"Nothing suspicious about the family shoveling the snow" the white coated man said.

"True" spoke the one in the red coat with his arms in his pockets. "But that little one might make a tasty snack."

"We are not to engage anyone. So, no snacking on these humans." The other one snapped towards his comrade "Although I guess he would make a nice treat." The red coated one chuckled.

The griffin and fox were relieved that so far into their investigation they had not found anything suspicious about this quiet town. It seemed like a simple town where everyone knew everyone, and they all got along in their own way of life. The creatures were also happy that their disguises were easily dismissed by those around them.

"It feels odd being here," The fox said in taking his hands out of his pockets.

"In this world?" The griffin asked turning to his comrade.

"In these bodies, they feel right but at the same time they don't feel like us." The fox said twisting its fingers which it was never able to do before.

"I agree with you on that one, it does feel weird having to keep my wings under wraps like this. They're starting to ache."

"Well, we'll just have to tough it out. The sooner we get back home the sooner you can stretch your wings and I can have my paws back."

MICHAEL MCGEE

The two creatures, turned human, resumed their reconnaissance. A tall girl with bright blue hair strolled past them, nothing suspicious about that. The girl who she was recently talking to however, something looked different about her. There was something within her that the creatures could see. It was faint, almost not there at all, but it was still there. A glow. The creatures could see a very faint glow within the heart of that human girl who strolled across the field. No other human in the area had that effect.

"What do you think about that one?" The fox asked quietly not taking his orange eyes off the girl.

"There is definitely something unique about her," The griffin said.

"Do you think she should be someone we should report to Zeus?"

"Let's just follow her from a distance for now, once we figure out which house, she lives in we can observe the areas around that place. That might give us more information."

The humans moved from the tree and strolled off towards the girl. They kept an eye over their surroundings. Looking for signs of anything that might indicate the whereabouts of what they searched for. The girl kept walking along and didn't look back which made the creatures relax a fraction. Soon she arrived at a small house and went in without delay. The fox and griffin looked around the area, certain this was where the human lived. Houses ran along the street, some children played in a nearby field, a forest ran up the side of a mountain. It seemed like just an ordinary neighborhood for the humans. Not wanting to draw attention to themselves by standing

ANGEL OF DARKNESS

around in one place for too long the creatures decided to leave. Promising themselves that they would keep an eye on that young girl.

The next day brought sun for the small mountain town. The light flickering off the snow. It was just another day in a quite mountain town. The fox and griffin walked along the sidewalk. They had stayed in the mountains for the night, hunted deer in the forest for a morning meal, and were back on patrol duty for their masters. Coming up to the house they had marked the previous day they saw the dark-haired girl walk out and head down the road. When they caught up to her the creatures stood by her near a bench where she was sitting. She didn't make much acknowledgment to their presence; she simply turned and gave them a quick smile as they arrived. A yellow transportation device the humans had crafted from metal arrived after a few minutes had passed. The creatures noticed the words "school bus" written upon the top. The black-haired girl hopped on, and it drove away leaving the other humans standing in the morning glow.

"We should probably follow that girl; there may be something we can learn if we find out where she's going," The fox said.

"Right, but the person commanding that bus did not let us on board," The griffin replied.

"Then we walk and follow the tracks it left behind," The fox said pointing to the ground where the snow had been parted into two lines.

The creatures followed the tracks for some time until they reached a large building where multiple humans were converging. There were hundreds of them. The two creatures cursed this problem, they had lost their target.

"There" the fox said quietly while pointing ahead. The dark-haired girl could be seen walking beside the blue haired girl the creatures had noticed the previous day. As they walked the creatures noticed that some of the other humans kept their distance. Many faces showed hints of fear or uncertainty. Three taller females however strolled up to the dark and blue haired girls and blocked their path. The creatures walked closer so they could overhear what was being said between the groups. A half circle of bystanders had converged around the area, obviously something was about to happen, and the observers knew they would have wanted to hear it.

"Listen Victoria, thinking you know the truth about Max doesn't give you any extra excuses to be tough." The dark-haired girl spoke.

"Oh, right like you know the truth?" Victoria said back "Get real, little Miss Problem Child here can't even act tough whenever her past is brought up."

The faces of the bystanders didn't change, they didn't even flinch.

"As a matter of fact, Victoria," the blue haired girl said loudly "I told Yuko the truth about my past the other day and she still accepts who I am regardless."

After the girl said that the crowd gasped. The griffin and fox remained in the back, off to the side, keeping an eye on the scene. The faint glow within the black-haired girl became slightly brighter.

"Can I ask what happened to you Max?" A boy in the front row asked, the girls turned around and after a

ANGEL OF DARKNESS

moment the black-haired girl whispered something to the blue haired one. "If you don't want to that's alright. I just think we all would like to know the truth." The boy said again.

"Is there anyone else here who would like to hear the truth?" The girl who the creatures assumed was Max said. Several hands went up, then a few more. The rest of the group stayed quiet and just slowly walked away. The creatures noticed that they were shrouded in fear for some reason. Knowing the truth to whatever happened to that girl had obviously caused them to be afraid, and it had happened after the dark-haired girl spoke to her. They stayed back, out of sight, and listened.

"I don't feel comfortable saying it out here, can we go inside?" Max asked.

"Sure, if you feel better that way." Another person in the group of bystanders replied.

"You three can come too if you want, it might make you come to your senses that I don't care anymore about what you have to say."

The creatures peaked around the corner and watched the group head inside; the black-haired girl's glow had not diminished. It remained brighter than it had been. That could not have been good.

"That girl, do you think she did something?" the griffin asked once they were alone.

"No doubt about it." The fox replied. "That girl had something to do with what just happened. The fear, the reactions, the uncertainty in their eyes; it all happened after that dark-haired girl spoke to that other human."

"I agree and I think we should inform Zeus about what we found."

"Do you think this is connected to that dark being we were informed of; the one we were instructed to stay away from?"

"It doesn't seem that this girl is the essence of that dark one, however she definitely has something about her that makes me wonder who she is."

"If that person is this dark being, it could be the glow she emitted within is what fuels her power, or at least hides her true form."

"But why a glow? That doesn't seem very dark."

"I'm unsure of that myself. Let's consult our master and see what he has to say about this, he may want us to bring that being to him for analysis into her power."

"Good idea. Let's get out of here first though I don't want that human to learn about what we are and what Zeus plans to do with her."

With that the creatures, still in human form, sped off towards the forest.

Zeus sat upon his throne; he was greatly concerned now. The Egyptian and Greek God's search of the world revealed several places shrouded in fear. The Egyptians made the search faster than anticipated, but still left no direct area with which to investigate. Their scouts had finally reported back and the news they brought did not repair Zeus' worry about their situation.

Picking up the purple crystal Hades gave him; Zeus spoke his brother's name. The purple gem rose and spun before opening a small portal where Zeus could see Hades rummaging through some shelves. Hades turned towards the portal a second later.

"Zeus" he said, "Have you learned anything new?"

"Our search of the world with the Egyptians turned up several new areas of darkness, but what is more important is what our scouts have informed me of."

"What did they find?"

"A girl, but she was different than the other mortals around her. She has a strange glow about her and those around her react in a strange way."

"What do you mean by a strange way?"

"They said fear spread to those around her and she seems to be able to control the actions of those around her without directly saying anything to them. The scouts said that she talked to another human and that they saw others around her react in fear shortly after that."

"Do they believe this girl may be the one we seek?"

"Perhaps, the creatures said that the glow within the girl was weak but became stronger just prior to the other humans becoming fearful of her."

"If what they reported is true then we may need to analyze this human further. If we brought her to Olympus the light that surrounds the kingdom may be enough to restrict her power. The other Olympians could standby in case something goes wrong, and we need to immobilize her."

"I don't want to put the other Olympians in danger."

"But you do want to learn more about this enemy we face. This girl may be the key."

MICHAEL MCGEE

Zeus pondered at that thought. He wanted to learn more about the dark being and if this girl was the key to learning more, he did not want to waste the chance. At the same time, he did not want his fellow Olympians from being harmed should this plan fail. But he felt that they may never get a better chance if opportunities like this, where their foe may be weaker than them, would pass by.

"Alright, I'll tell our creatures to capture the girl alive. Will you come here to Olympus with me when they arrive?" Zeus said.

"Yes, but for now I need to remain here, I still haven't' found anything but I know I'm close to a discovery." With that the portals closed, and Zeus prepared his mind to contact their creatures; hoping at the same time that he was not making a mistake.

Chapter Fifteen

THE SMALL GROUP of students, even the Sisters, was surprisingly quiet as Max told her story about the armed robbery. They didn't make any move to interrupt her or even criticize her when she stuttered at the end. Max did feel more confident thanks to Yuko's words outside the school. "Just take a deep breath and let it out." Yuko was sitting beside Max as the story was recited; she wanted to be supportive to her friend. When Max finished the room remained silent, which was odd considering they were in the music room. Victoria was the first to speak.

"I… I never thought it was that bad," She said to the stunned group. What they were stunned about remained a mystery. Was it the story or the fact that the leader of The

Sisters was the first to speak and not in a hurtful way?

"What did you think happened?" Max asked, "I thought you knew the whole story and that's why you always used it against me."

"I only knew that there was a gun involved in an event that you were also involved in and that you did something to make you paranoid. I never thought that you actually pulled the trigger on someone and killed them." Victoria hung her head after she said that. No one said a word for a few minutes, and then Ashley and Mandy both stood up.

"Max, Yuko" they said together "we are terribly sorry for what we've done to you over these past few weeks."

Max and Yuko looked at them for a moment. They seemed sincere in their apology. Max knew it would take a bit more than that to make her forgive them; Yuko was the same, but she was a bit more accepting of their apology.

"It's not much, but it's a start" Max said.

"What about you Victoria?" Yuko asked.

Victoria looked around the room, everyone was staring at her. Yuko sensed the other students in the room had been victims of Victoria and her gang in the past. Hopefully, no one got worse than Max did from them.

"I'm sorry as well." She said as she hung her head.

"Look up and tell us that." A girl in the group said.

"I'm sorry, for… for everything I did to you Max, Yuko, everyone here." Victoria said looking everyone in the eye. Several students nodded in acknowledgement. Others turned away and looked back towards Max, they obviously didn't feel like accepting an apology at the moment from

ANGEL OF DARKNESS

Victoria.

"Does anyone else know what happened to you Max?" the girl in the group asked.

"Including this small group, there are about 12 people who know the full truth. What do all of you think about it?" Max said.

"It sounds like it was terrible." A boy, who Yuko recognized as John from the other day, asked. "I can't imagine what that must have been like."

"Same here," several other students said one after the other.

"Is there anything we can do to help you now?" John asked.

"If you could stop being afraid of me every time my name comes up in conversations, or if you see me around the school, I think that might be a helpful place to start," Max replied.

"Several other students have already begun to do that with us" Yuko said. "It seems like it's having an effect on those around us as other students are slowly recognizing that Max is a good person despite her past."

"I guess that's the least we can do for now." Ashley said, "If it can help you forgive us for what we've done to you then you have my support."

"Same here," Mandy followed.

"I'll help you as well." Victoria said "I feel really guilty now that I know the full truth. If anyone should be trying to be better, it should be me."

The whole room echoed with words of agreement. Yuko

looked towards Max who was looking over the group. She was proud of her friend for coming forward and revealing her tragedy, at least to a small group.

The bell rang so the group got up and headed out of the music room. Everyone stayed quiet Max and Yuko both agreed that the story had impacted them in some way, even the Sisters were quiet as they walked out. The expressions on the group's faces showed their still surprised thoughts. Max wasn't convinced that Victoria's and her gang's attempt at an apology was significant.

"So, what did you think about their apology?" Yuko asked.

"It's definitely going to take more than a 'sorry for everything' to make up for what they've done to me."

"At least they attempted to make amends."

"Yeah, I guess that's something new for them."

The two strolled off to their morning classes. Math class was uneventful; they only worked on quadratic equations which were a mind boggle for both Max and Yuko. Construction class was next; Yuko was able to finish sanding down her cabinet and was ready to stain it for a final touch. Max had finished two of the legs for her table and was also sanding them down as the class ended for the day. Social class was next for Yuko while Max had forensics. It was a half day, so they were released from school at noon. Yuko felt like taking a walk through the forest to get some fresh air and relax from the struggles of life for a bit.

The bell rang half an hour later and Yuko strolled off to the second floor where the forensics class was in the computer room looking up decay rates in relation to insect population surrounding deceased bodies. Max strolled out and Yuko asked her if she wanted to join her on her nature walk. Max agreed, also needing some fresh air after opening to more students about her past.

As the two friends walked out of the school, the two humans who were observing the area nearby watched the girl's movements.

"When do we make our move?" The fox said as he observed the glow from the girl walking across the street.

"When she is alone and there is no one else around, you heard Zeus, we are not supposed to let others see us." The griffin replied.

"The glow has receded within her. Wasn't it shining more brilliantly a while ago before she entered the building?"

"It was yes, but that doesn't matter now. We have our orders, and we have to carry out our master's will. He wants the girl alive."

"That might be difficult as she has someone with her right now."

"Let's follow them for now. Eventually they will have to separate."

"That sounds like the only thing we can do for now; but what if they don't separate?"

"Then we will have to think of another option."

The griffin and fox moved to trail the girls before they were lost from view. They didn't find anything odd about their targets' movements. They walked just like normal humans and were talking about something as they walked.

If this was the target their masters were afraid of; it was blending in with the society of humans extraordinarily well. The glow seemed to be fluctuating every so often within the smaller girl; which made the creatures' question what the glow even was.

"Perhaps it's the eminence of her power?" the fox said as they moved through the field of snow.

"Perhaps, but if that's true, what is she releasing through that power?" the griffin said, keeping his eyes up. "More importantly though, look at where they're heading." The fox looked up and saw that they were heading towards the forest that rested at the base of one of the mountains.

"If they get too far ahead of us, we'll lose them." The griffin said.

"What do we do then? We can't reveal ourselves to them."

"It looks like we may not have much of a choice."

"Look if this girl is the one our master seeks, it might be a bad idea to let her get into that forest, it looks pretty dark within the trees which may only increase the girl's power. I think that the glow is what contains her power until she's within the shadows. Think about it."

A being of shadow, a faint put powerful glow, the glow goes down when in the sunlight.

The griffin looked up just to confirm his thoughts, clouds were rolling in, but the sun still shone brightly in the sky. "That makes sense, if this girl she is with is a target herself, it would make sense to try and get her into an area where she will be weaker or at a disadvantage. But why this other mortal?"

ANGEL OF DARKNESS

"I don't know, let's just get both of them and take them to the bosses; we'll explain our theory to them and if this other girl turns out to be nothing of use then our masters can just erase her memory."

Max and Yuko walked along the snow-covered ground, the air was cool from the wind which blew around them and there were some rain warnings being issued for the town.

"First snow, now rain, seems the weather can't make up its mind" Max said rubbing her hands.

"It definitely a bit colder than it was this morning." Yuko said, putting her hands in her pockets.

"Excuse me" they heard someone say.

Turning around Max and Yuko saw two men standing behind them, where they had come from both girls had no idea.

"Can we help you?" Max asked, looking serious.

"We were wondering if you had some time to spare, our boss would like to talk to the two of you for a while," the man on the right side.

"Who's this boss of yours?" Max said, glancing towards Yuko who saw worry in her eyes.

"The police chief of this town" the man on the left said after a minute where he looked towards the other man. Yuko felt Max take hold of her hand. Yuko sensed Max was incredibly nervous.

"If you are police officers, where are your uniforms and badges?"

Both men remained silent for a moment. 'Well, that was

great improvisation' they heard in their minds.

'Zeus,' they asked with their minds.

'Yes, now stop making things up that are too obvious to those two and bring them to me before they get away.'

'As you wish,' the creatures replied.

"Look, our boss is a very powerful man, and he thinks you might be able to help him, now please come with us." The man on the right said before extending his hand. Max quickly hit the arm away and instantly turned and began sprinting towards the forest with Yuko being dragged along.

"Nice going" the fox said as the griffin moved his arm back.

"Police officers without badges, great idea" the griffin replied. "Well come on." With that he began sprinting towards the forest after the girls with his companion close behind.

Yuko and Max sprinted through the trees; the sunlight was being interrupted by the snow sitting on the trees making it difficult to see where they were running.

"Max slow down," Yuko called.

"No way, this doesn't feel right, and I don't want to experience another case of being harmed in my life." Max replied as she pulled Yuko along. "Trust me, we don't know who those men are, and we don't know what they will do to us if we go with them to this boss they speak of."

Yuko instinctively knew Max was worried from the minute she grabbed her hand. She felt the same way. Something did not feel right about this situation. If being

ANGEL OF DARKNESS

pursued by two people she didn't know wasn't enough, the forest also seemed different. How she sensed that Yuko had no idea, but something was telling her that they shouldn't have ran into the trees. Lost in thought Yuko forgot to look down at her feet and tripped over a large root, taking Max down with her.

"You alright?" Max asked.

"Yeah I'm fine, sorry."

"Come on we can lose them if we keep going."

A snap behind them was all they needed to know just how wrong Max was. The two men came out of the trees behind them, stopping before them.

"Look this isn't what you think," the man in the red said.

Max got up and stood in front of Yuko, arms raised, fists tight. "Yeah right, this isn't what it looks like. Who the hell are you?"

"Look here's the truth" the man in the white coat said, "We think your friend behind you may be using you."

"Using me?"

"Yes, we've been observing the two of you and we believe she isn't what she appears to be."

Max glanced towards Yuko who quickly shook her head rapidly. "Why should I listen to you?"

"This may sound crazy to you, but it's the truth" the red coated man said, "Our bosses are the God of the Sky Zeus, and God of the Dead Hades."

The four in the area remained silent, no one said a word, and they just stared at each other. The red coated man had his arms up trying to appear peaceful. The white coated man had his face in his hand as if he couldn't believe that their cover was blown just like that. Max looked like she was ready to fight, but also had a hint of surprise in her eyes.

Yuko was shocked *Hades? This is almost the same as my dream, but that's just it, it was a dream, this can't be real. Can it?*

Max suddenly burst out laughing, breaking the silence. "Get real" she said, "You really expect us to believe that two Gods from the Greek mythological tales are your bosses?"

"I can't believe you just said that" the white coated man said looking towards the other man. "Now we don't have a choice." He said as his body began emanating a white aura.

"What choice did we have, they wanted the truth and that's the truth."

"Look we tried doing it calmly and that didn't work, it's time to try a new method."

"I guess you're right, your boss Zeus is at least a bit wiser than Hades so I guess he could have made you reasonably smarter than me" the red coated man said as he began emanating a red aura.

"Hades is going to have you burn for eternity for that."

"Whatever; let's just get this done."

Both girls watched in horror and shock as the men before them began to change. Their bodies were enveloped in light and flame. From the light the girls saw two wings spread out, a tail and two clawed legs followed suit. An eagle headed creature with wings stood in the light a moment later. From the flames came a four-legged creature, the flames surrounding it converged and merged into the

ANGEL OF DARKNESS

body of a creature, which resembled a fox, which was bathed in flames along its back and snout.

"What in God's name!?" Max screamed as Yuko slowly got to her feet. She couldn't believe it; she couldn't even think. Her dream; was it coming true?

"My master Hades wants to see you" the fox spoke in a deep voice. "You will not escape this time creature of darkness!"

Yuko quickly grabbed Max's hand and ran through the trees. She ran faster than she had ever run before. Not thinking; not even breathing, just sprinting. This couldn't be real. It couldn't. But there was no denying what she just saw. Nothing mattered at this point, not the snow, not the trees, not the fact that her dream was coming true. All that mattered was getting herself and her friend away from these creatures.

Chapter Sixteen

HADES RUMMAGED THROUGH his study, his dark eyes scanning every book and paper on the shelf. Something was wrong he knew it; there was a reason for that dark being entering the Underworld. He had already searched his gate extensively and found nothing wrong with it. That creature had gotten past the gate somehow and Hades had no understanding of how that could have happened. Hades turned to gaze outside to rest his eyes for a minute. Watching the souls below him scream in pain. Torrents of flame erupted out of the depths of despair and suffering. Cerberus paced along the walkways keeping one face fixed on his master. Hades sensed his worry. For the dead souls it was just another day in the Underworld; but for Hades and

Cerberus it was anything but.

As Hades turned to leave a torrent of flame erupted outside his window, illuminating the room in a red light. For a moment Hades caught sight of a faint object in the corner of the room. A book lay hidden in the shadows. One that was pitch black. Turning the pages Hades quickly knew what this book was. Reaching the page he needed, his face instantly turned to shock and realization.

"Of course," Hades said out loud. "I don't have much time." With that Hades quickly released a massive amount of energy and catapulted himself towards Olympus. He only hoped his brother had not acted out of fear and ordered their servants to act before consulting him.

Zeus paced within the grand chamber of Olympus. The creatures had revealed their true forms and he was not pleased with that, but his fear and worry controlled him. He was sure this girl they pursued was connected to the dark shadow of their past. The past had caught up to the future and was about to come true unless he stepped in and stopped it. That girl was the only being around the world who they had found, except for the known Demigods of the world, which was different from the other humans. That's what made her a target, a target with unknown powers, and Zeus was scared of what she could possibly do.

"ZEUS!!!!" a loud roar suddenly erupting within the chamber called out.

Zeus stepped back as a torrent of shadow erupted within the chamber and Hades emerged with intense speed.

"Hades what is it?" Zeus said.

"I figured it out. I know why that creature came into the

ANGEL OF DARKNESS

Underworld."

"How did you..."

"Read this!" Hades said thrusting a black book at Zeus.

Zeus looked at the book before turning the pages. It appeared to be a journal. Pages filled with depictions of creatures holding great power. One page began discussing a being who brought fear to all those who gaze upon it. A person of terrible power. Turning the page Zeus saw that the book suddenly cut off and now talked about a small, winged creature with sharp claws.

"I don't understand; why does it change?"

"That's just it." Hades said, "It cuts off because pages are missing."

"What even is this?"

"It's a record book I use to keep track of all the creatures and beings that have ever served under me or are under my command."

"What are within those missing pages?"

"Those pages depict the being who I told you about previously. The servant whose power I was able to take before he left my service."

"You believe that shadow took these pages because it wanted to learn about a previous servant of yours?"

"You don't understand. He was one the strongest and most feared beings I had ever seen. Just looking at him brought fear to anyone. He was able to control darkness in ways I have never known before."

"Control darkness?"

"Not only that but he was able to cancel out the powers of those around him. I never understood how he was able to do that, but some of his power that I took from him is how my gate can disrupt energy around it. That power comes from that dark entity."

"This being, what was his name?"

"I told you I swore I would never say that creatures name again. Now that I'm thinking about it, you haven't ordered our creatures to do anything have you? We need to take a different approach at looking at this target they have found, we need to analyze more closely how she affects those around her."

"I just ordered them to capture the girls, they've just began the chase."

"You fool!! I told you to contact me before you did anything." Hades yelled turning towards the center of the chamber. Walking to the center he looked down where he could see the mortal world below him. Fixing his mind on his servant his view was instantly taken to it. The fox ran through a forest with the griffin behind it. Two girls rushed through the forest ahead of them. Hades pulled his gaze back to get a view of where they were running. Shadows covered the trees. Hades sensed something was wrong.

"Zeus, we need them to halt their assault."

"What, why, we are so close."

"This doesn't feel right; we need to contact them now. Tell them to retreat from the forest and to not kill those girls. I sense it, something very powerful is down there."

The fox ran through the trees, his flames licked the wood from the damp trees. These girls were thinner than he and

ANGEL OF DARKNESS

the griffin were so they couldn't take the tight gaps between the trees like the girl could. The forest also grew darker as they ran deeper into the maze of trees.

"Can you…me?" the fox suddenly heard. He stopped his chase; the griffin did the same.

"Did you hear that?" the griffin asked.

"Don't…the girls…stop…them…to powerful."

"Sounds like Zeus wants us to stop the girls, she must be stronger than we thought." The griffin said.

"…Kill…"

"Kill?" the fox asked.

They waited a minute but got no reply. The fox turned to face the griffin. "What do you think?"

"It sounds like Zeus wants us to kill the child. She must be stronger than we imagined."

"Why the sudden change of plans?"

"Perhaps Hades returned from the Underworld and found something that confirms their suspicion. This child must be their enemy."

"So, we finish them off?"

"That is our master's word, and his word is our bond."

"Alright, let's find our prey."

The fox and griffin rushed through the forest to pick up the scent of where their prey had run off too. Zeus looked down at them watching them continue their pursuit.

"What did you tell them?" Hades asked, also watching the pursuit.

"I told them that to leave the girls alone. They were not to kill them; just retreat, there is something powerful down there and we don't know what it was."

Hades looked down at the forest again. His eyes grew wide. "Zeus…look at the forest."

Zeus looked down at the forest as instructed. It was dark, covered in white snow, but still dark. Then he saw it. A mist. A black mist covered the trees, shrouding the forest in darkness. "What is that?"

"I knew it." Hades spoke softly.

"You knew what?"

"The shadowed being that entered my realm, it took those pages from that book to gain knowledge about how to control the darkness. I took notes on what I observed within the power I stole from my servant after I got my gate up. The shadow is there, in the forest. It was there the whole time. It's controlling the darkness and preventing us from communicating with our creatures."

Zeus looked down in horror. Their enemy had been right in front of them the entire time and they never saw it.

"We have to warn them." Zeus said, "We have to get those girls and our creatures out of there."

"We can't!" Hades said before Zeus could do anything. "I recognize that aura; it's the same as what emanates through my gate. It's impossible to pass through it."

"We have to try!" Zeus said filled with fear. Calling lightning to his side he threw the bolt down to Earth, he needed to do something to get their creatures attention. Zeus watched as the bolt traveled towards the forest, but it never breached the clouds. The bolt simply died in the air. "What happened?"

"The bolt suddenly stopped." Hades said also surprised.

"That's impossible."

"That darkness is much stronger than what I have within my gate. It may even be stronger than us."

"That cannot be!" Zeus said as he conjured up his strength and teleported himself down to the world below. He returned a minute later. "I can't get into the forest. The shadows are protecting it."

"Zeus there is nothing we can do."

"There has to be something!"

"Brother, we cannot enter that area, the darkness is too strong." Hades said before turning back and looking down at the trees below. "So strong I believe it may be connected to the one who previously served me."

Hades remained quiet for a minute before muttering quietly "The dreaded Hand of Death himself."

Zeus looked towards his brother; fear had enveloped both their eyes.

"There is nothing we can do," Hades said "We just have to watch. Watch and learn." With that Hades vanished in a cloud of shadow as he returned to the Underworld. Zeus sat down and continued to glance at the world below. He feared for what he and his brother were about to see.

Chapter Seventeen

MAX AND YUKO dashed forward. The darkness around them made it very difficult to find their way through the forest. Stopping behind a large tree they began to try and catch their breath.

"Think we lost them?" Yuko panted.

"For now," Max said painfully.

"What were those creatures?"

"They looked like a griffin and some sort of fox."

"A fox of flame. Same as my dream."

"I hate to admit it, but there may be something in those dreams that was real after all."

"Do you think they're real now after seeing that?" Yuko said glancing around the tree.

"Who?"

"The Gods of the Greek mythological tales?"

"After seeing two humans turn into massive creatures that started chasing us. I'm ready to believe anything today." Max sat down trying to rest. "I still think that's crazy."

"I'm with you there." Yuko said also taking a seat. "But at the same time, I'm thinking it might be true."

"Ok… we can talk about that crazy thought after we get out of here."

"How do you expect us to do that? This forest keeps getting darker the deeper we go."

"I don't know, but we'll have to figure out something."

"This feels like I'm back in my dreams, only it's real this time."

"Do you ever get away in your dream?"

"No, I always get caught and then wake up screaming. The dreams seem to end short, but always end with hints towards death."

"There has to be a way we can get out of here."

"Well, that's all I know. My dreams end in death for me. However last time I thought I saw someone else in the forest with me, I don't know what or who it was. I just saw a silhouette. I bet you think that's pretty-" Yuko began before Max placed a hand over her mouth to silence her.

Placing a finger to her own mouth Max pointed silently

to the left before taking her hand away from Yuko. Yuko turned and saw the flames from the fox dancing along the darkness. A moment later the fox emerged, sniffing the ground, trying to pick up the girl's scent. Max pointed to the right and mouthed 'this way.'

The two of them slowly rose from their hiding place and quietly moved away from the fox. Not being able to see made their escape difficult and Max unintentionally stepped on a fallen branch. The fox's ears perked up as it brought its head back up. Turning its head, the fox looked right at the girls. It was dark so they thought they were safe, but then the fox put its head down and growled slightly.

"Run" Yuko said before taking off through the trees. Turning her head, she saw Max close behind her as the fox rushed through the trees after them. The flames on its back grew and its speed intensified. Yuko and Max fled down two different paths and the fox pursued Yuko the heat radiating off it began to catch her back as she began to slow down from exhaustion.

Stopping and turning around she decided to face the creature, maybe she could find a way out of the situation if she replicated her dream but tried to change the end. The fox also stopped, just like it had in the dream, and both beings stared at each other.

"What do you want?" Yuko asked the fox as the flames began to slowly melt the snow around them.

"I want to follow my master's orders. There is something about you that makes you different from other humans. My master figured it out. You are the one who entered his realm and disrupted the balance that he and his brothers have worked so hard to achieve. I don't know why you don't call your power forward to protect yourself. I guess you just don't want to scare your friend."

"What are you talking about? I never entered any realm; I don't know what you're talking about. Who are your master's brothers?"

"Zeus, God of the Sky, and Poseidon, God of the Seas."

"You mean to tell me that those beings from myths and legends are real?"

"They are."

So far her plan of stalling seemed to be working, but Yuko was still shocked that those beings were apparently real. If this wasn't a dream then there was no way to deny that; especially since there was a fox on fire standing a few feet away from her. "You said I was the being of darkness. What does that mean?"

"That I will not answer because you already what I speak of," the fox said as it lowered itself closer to the ground. "And you won't escape my master this time" the fox roared as it rushed towards the girl, tossing flames forward from its tail.

Yuko tried to dodge the creature but the flames that preceded it cut off escapes from the sides. The fox landed on top of her; pressing down hard on her chest. Her eyes filled with fear, her dream had become real, and nothing could stop it now. Glancing off to the side, not wanting to look the beast in the eye Yuko saw something through the flames. A second later an object was swung at the fox's face. The connection was enough to throw the creature off Yuko who panted as she tried to focus on whom or what helped her.

ANGEL OF DARKNESS

"Guess your dreams didn't show you that," Max said as she helped Yuko up with her free hand. A thick tree branch held in her other. "Come on."

Yuko and Max escaped through the trees as the fox got to its feet. Hearing a loud growl behind them got the girls thinking at the same time. 'Where was the griffin?'

Their question was answered almost instantly as the winged creature crashed through the trees before them. Both girls stopped as the griffin turned towards them, its eagle eyes fixed upon them. A moment later the fox emerged from behind them, blood seeped from its nose.

"Time to finish this," the griffin said as it swung its wing around the clearing it had made. Both Yuko and Max were blown back as the air rushed towards them. Landing on the ground Yuko quickly got to her feet. Grabbing the tree trunk that Max had dropped she rushed at the griffin but was easily stopped by its large claws cutting her arm. She fell to the ground as the fox leapt over Max to join the griffin. Both looked down at Yuko.

"Funny, I guess hiding who she truly was is too important for this girl," The fox said.

Yuko turned; blood dripped from her arm. The griffin brought its claws up and swung them towards her. Yuko shut her eyes quickly to try and brace for the pain. She heard a scream echo through the area. Only her mouth had stayed tightly shut. Opening her eyes, she instantly froze. Max was standing above her, four claws piercing her body.

"Max?" Yuko weakly said.

Max looked down at Yuko, a weak smile on her face. "I don't care who they say you are. Being of darkness or whatever, you are my friend.

"No… you… you can't"

"Thank you for…" Max breathed as she coughed up blood. She opened her mouth to say more; but never did, she just smiled. Then Max went still.

The griffin reared back its head as it screeched in triumph at its kill. Yuko was frozen in place, unable to move, unable to breathe. Her friend had just been killed and it looked like she was next. The fox swiped her with its tail, knocking what little air she had out of her body as she was flung towards a tree. Hitting it she felt her leg connect behind her body, the bone shattered. Now she was completely helpless. The griffin turned on her as the fox moved in to finish her off. Both creatures pounced at her helpless body. Shutting her eyes tight, Yuko tried to brace for the outstretched claws of the creatures. But they never came.

She waited and waited.

Then a screech of anger shot out of the darkness. Yuko opened her eyes and looked in shock. A shadow had appeared in front of her and was blocking the creatures; they clawed viciously at the darkness but could not penetrate its form. The shadows in the area seemed to converge around the tree, shielding the girl from harm. As her attackers began to circle the ring of darkness that protected her, Yuko saw a new shape begin to form from the shadows around her. The trees began to sway in the wind as their grounded image collected before the girl. A being of night rose from the ground, the form was unrecognizable. It was a silhouette of what appeared to be a human with what looked like long strands of hair tied into

ANGEL OF DARKNESS

two ponytails on either side of the head; which blew calmly in the wind. The figure moved forward towards the girl lying under the tree as it lowed what Yuko assumed to be the face closer to her own. Moving beside her head, Yuko heard four words. Words that were faint and distant.

"You are the one."

Yuko froze. Her eyes wide and her limbs cold. As the figure moved back, it lowered itself to Yuko's chest. Headfirst; it slowly entered her body. With her entire body paralyzed, all Yuko could do was watch in horror as the shadow faded within her. She felt it pierce her heart like a slowly drawn blade. As the feet entered, Yuko's body became stiff. She screamed in agony as her body was torn from her soul. Her eyes saw fire, her body became lifeless. Her mind raced in fear, afraid of what was happening to her. As her screams became louder the creatures whose onslaught was still stalled by the shadows began to fear what they saw.

The girl's clothing was torn from her body, shattering into complete darkness that began to rise and grow into a new form. The girl watched as the night that was once her clothes twisted and blended into something else. The shadows combined and produced a new form of darkness. A cloak as black as the darkest night. It draped itself over the girl as the shadows encircled her injured leg and arm beginning to remove the pain they were causing. Yuko's body rose as she felt new energy surge through her body, new strength like nothing she'd ever known was surging through her entire being.

As she stood on her resurrected legs, she felt a connection to the darkness around her. The shadowy walls dropped and surrounded her waist as a belt and sword hilt were generated from their form. Her instincts suddenly kicked in. Yuko gripped the handle and drew her new blade. A blade that was pale white, not the normal white of clouds or pale skin, but a stark white that showed no life within. The color of death itself.

The strengthened warrior turned to face her attackers who were rooted in place by the figure before them. She suddenly saw new truth about the creatures, their weakness. Through her eyes she saw where the blade needed to pierce its target. With her instincts guiding her, Yuko charged towards the creatures as they rose to face her. The fox moved fast as the griffin rose to gain a height advantage. Yuko moved fast, faster than anything the creatures could see. Within the blink of an eye the girl had landed on the back of the fox and pierced her sword into the creatures neck, swinging the sword forward, Yuko reared the foxes head up as its muzzle was sliced in two. Placing her feet onto the back of the now lifeless demon, the warrior faced its next target. The griffin expanded its wings. Channeled pure energy, neither solar nor electric, into its body. Rearing back the griffin released this power at the burning face of its enemy.

Raise the sword!

Yuko raised the blade and took the entire attack head on; the area was singed into ashes and dust as the sword collided with the beam. As it breathed heavily at its lack of strength, the creature looked at the smoke that rose from the area of impact.

At first it saw nothing, then a light. A bright light shone through the night. The griffin stared at the blinding light trying to make sense of what happened, and then it saw the glow. A blue glow. A flame of terror engulfed the area. The warrior stood unharmed atop the fried corpse of her first victim. The blade glowed with all colors of light and dark. The griffin then realized that the sword hadn't just diverted the attack. It had absorbed all the energy. The terror of the skies was now helpless as that attack expanded its strength. The warrior of the night leapt at the creature and drove her blade into the very heart of the beast. It screeched in agony as the intolerable pain engulfed what little soul it had. It fell in a crash so strong a city would have shaken.

As clouds rolled in overhead, the warrior rose from beneath the griffin's wings. Standing on her now fully strengthened legs, Yuko walked towards the lifeless being that was once her friend. As rain showered down over the two, Yuko knelt. Staring into the face of the being, she lowered a hand and closed the open eyes so that her body could rest free from the soul. The water gathered into a puddle that reflected the truth towards the new girl. As Yuko gazed at herself she became entranced. Her skin had gone pale, lacking color similar to the bloodstained sword in her hand. Her eyes had stayed blue but her left one was covered by what looked like blue flame. The tail on the edge of her eye moved and swayed in the wind. It appeared to hide her true self, replacing her frail human face with one of mystery. Her cloak and hood had draped her entire being in a color of pure darkness. She stared at her burning eye, hot, but causing no pain. As the flame died down and faded within her, she stared at her new body and then towards the sky.

The Gods had done this to her friend. If they were real, then they had to be stopped. They caused destruction with their desire for power over mortals; Yuko was sure that this anger and fear that caused them to target her and her friend wasn't over yet.

"What are you?" she asked towards the shadows.

There was no answer, only a feeling of sadness and sorrow.

"Who are you?"

"One who knows how to get your friend back" a distant voice spoke softly in her head.

"Get her back?"

"Help me, and I will help you."

She gave no response. As Yuko walked away, the shadows crept towards her, gifting her with new strength. She smirked as she felt her new abilities flow through her and walked off into the night.

Chapter Eighteen

ZEUS STOOD IN the grand chamber of Olympus. Paralyzed. One thought ran through his mind. *How? How could he have been so blind.*

The enemy was directly below them on the moral world the entire time and he had not noticed it.

"Zeus" a voice called against the silence.

Zeus turned and saw Hades standing there beside him. "The pillars of the Underworld, they are out of control." Hades said facing his stunned brother.

"I failed us brother."

"No, you did not. No one could have foreseen this."

"We could have," Zeus said before sitting down with his hands in his knees. "The Ancients showed us what was to come, we knew about it before it began, we should have acted sooner."

"What they showed us has nothing to do with what has just occurred. The shadow has only awoken, and we don't even know if this is the one we foresaw."

Hades knelt beside his brother before saying "For now, we must warn the others."

Zeus looked at Hades, Hades' dead eyes reflecting the light from his own. Without a word he nodded.

Odin walked the halls of Asgard's castle, the light shone brightly through the windows. "Another calm day in the nine realms" he said aloud through the chambers. As he walked Odin was calm and collected.

There was nothing to fear, peace was established after years of conflict, and the worlds were united. This was Odin's thought, until he felt something surge through his being.

"Loki!" he exclaimed before rushing through the halls. Reaching the throne room; he saw Loki sitting on the stairwell leading to the throne, twirling his knife on one finger. "Loki?"

"Hello father" the God of mischief said turning to face Odin. Loki was well known for his illusions; it was never known if the real one stood before you when facing him. Through his eye of wisdom, however, Odin saw that this was not an illusion. The real Loki sat before him.

"You were not the cause?" Odin asked his son in surprise.

"Cause of what?" Loki said grasping his knife.

ANGEL OF DARKNESS

"Oh… nothing," Odin replied before thinking *if it wasn't Loki then what was that just now?*

"Hello brother," Thor said towards Loki as he entered through one of the side halls. "Hello father."

"Thor, you're here as well?" Odin said.

"Yes, why would I not be?"

"He thinks that one of us was out causing trouble." Loki answered turning to Thor.

"That's rich coming from you brother" Thor chuckled. Loki looked towards Thor before putting on a false smile. "Why would there be trouble in these times father?"

Odin looked towards Thor; his face was calm "it's nothing Thor, I just had a chill a moment ago, thought Loki was up to his old tricks again. Nothing to worry about though."

As the doors to the main hall burst open, and Heimdall came rushing in, Odin wished he has not said that.

Heimdall rushed forwards before resting and holding his hands with his legs to catch his breath. "Lord Odin…" he gasped "I bring urgent news."

"What is it?"

"Jotunheim… it's cracked."

The three Gods gasped.

"Cracked?... How is that possible?" Loki asked with both anger and shock.

"I don't know. All I know is that there was silence and then the sound of ice being shattered echoed through the stars."

"I'm going there" Thor exclaimed before spinning Mjolnir in his hand.

"Thor wait!" Odin cried as Thor cast his hammer through the city towards the Bifrost, the hammer carrying him with great speed. "Blast!!" Odin exclaimed as the wind blew in his face.

"I'm going too. Jotunheim is my homeland I need to see it" Loki said before hurrying off to catch Thor. Odin quickly realized that there was no stopping them.

Facing Heimdall he asked, "Was there anything else that you noticed?"

"Nothing." Heimdall replied. "What could have caused the world of ice to split?"

"I don't know, this is unheard of." Odin said before thinking of another possibility "Could it be one of the stones?"

"Those have been lost for centuries so I cannot believe it was one of them."

The hall remained silent as the two beings pondered the reasoning behind this event.

"Could it be…" Odin said amid the silence.

"What?"

"Do you recall when the Greek Gods came here?"

"I do."

"Well, this is just a thought but what if…" Odin started before Hugin rushed into the chamber screaming loudly. "Hugin what is it?"

The bird landed on Odin's spear before crying loudly

ANGEL OF DARKNESS

"The Greek Gods of Earth, they are calling an emergency meeting, all beings must attend immediately!"

"How did you hear this?" Odin asked the raven.

"The Messenger God, Hermes, came rushing though the cosmos, calling all who could hear him to appear on Olympus at once."

The windows above the entrance burst apart as Thor crashed through them. Loki being carried by the clothing around his neck. Landing and tossing Loki to the ground Thor cried out "Father, the frost giants, they are unharmed, but their world is destroyed."

"What is the damage?" Odin asked quickly.

"Mountains of ice…reduced…to shards!" Loki said between gasps for air. "The ground is split apart."

"It can't be?" Odin said his face turning to sudden shock. "We leave for Olympus at once!"

"Olympus?" Thor and Loki asked in unison.

"The Greeks have called us to their domain immediately."

Loki and Thor turned to each other. They didn't say a word but through their time together they each knew what the other was thinking. It was not good.

Hades, Zeus, Poseidon, Athena, Ares, and Hermes all sat in the grand chamber.

"I ran to all the worlds known to us" Hermes said amid the silence "Others will come."

Zeus nodded silently.

In unison both light and darkness spawned within the

chamber. Odin, Thor, Loki and Heimdall emerged from the pillar of light. From the flames of shadow appeared Anubis with Ma'at at his side. Ra emerged from flames of light a moment later. Chronos arrived shortly after Sobek, who splashed through a pillar of water, as ripples in time brought its keeper to the present.

Once all Gods were present, Zeus addressed them to sit around the chamber. Everyone took their seats without question.

Hades stood to address those around him "We have called you here for one purpose and one purpose only." He said glancing around the room "To tell you that the time of darkness has arrived."

"Is it what we feared?" Anubis asked.

Hades stared into the God's emerald eyes before saying "It is."

"Then there is no time to waste" Ma'at spoke.

"That being you spoke of?" Odin asked towards the Greek brothers "is it real?"

Poseidon turned to face Odin "It is real, and it was awoken."

The chamber remained silent before Hades spoke again. "Those who do not believe us; look upon the truth" he said before pointing down at the mortal land below.

The Gods did as instructed. They saw a forest amid a mountain range. The forest was dark; shadows covered the trees, the earth, the roots. Amid the shadows however there was something which could be seen. A mortal by the looks of it, cloaked in darkness, a blue flame emanating from its body. The shadows collected around the being; following its will.

"So, it is true?" Chronos spoke as he watched.

"How can you be so certain?" Ra asked rising his head to face the Greeks.

"There is no other explanation." Hades said towards the Sun God. "This being, she is something else; something never seen before."

"I agree" Ma'at said turning to face the attendees. "Observe." With that she raised the Scales of Balance and held them towards the image of the one below them. The scales began tilting rapidly, continuously, furiously. The other items glowed with power as Anubis transferred his power to Ma'at. The scales came to rest shortly after. "The light which surrounds us shields us from her power, yet the darkness is still immensely strong."

"What should be call this creature?" Loki asked, "One with no name is one with no identity."

"There is only one name that fits this foe." Zeus spoke out causing all the Gods to turn towards him.

"And what name would fit this female mortal who walks below us?" Anubis asked calmly.

Zeus glanced around the room once more, then below to the surface. Silence enveloped the chamber before Zeus looked up and called out the name.

"The Angel of Darkness!"

All Gods glanced around the room, that name did fit what they saw. Zeus rose from his throne before making one last call.

"The Angel of Darkness has awoken. May The Ancients

guide us against this foe."

Epilogue

AS THE DARKNESS spread, Gods across the worlds could feel the power of the shadows surge through them. There was one however, who felt it the most. Within the clouds, where no light reached, a figure flew in the night. A God who was said to be the very incarnation of death itself, with wings blacker than the night before the dawn.

The faceless creature flew in the night looking for prey to feed on. Then it felt a presence, one that made the souls within his wings cry in fear. The circuits within his dark feathers reacted to a power that only he could feel, only he could sense, only he recognized. The power of the shadows which penetrated his spirit caused the figure to pause. Held in place as his wings glowed with power.

MICHAEL MCGEE

The God whose face was lifeless, showed no sign of fear, pity, happiness, or hope. It was said that this face never changed, always stole hope out of whomever gazed upon him. As the light from his wings faded, The Hand of Death looked down, as his still expression curled into a smile.

About the Author

Michael is a Canadian fantasy author from Edmonton Alberta. Michael's mental health condition, Asperger's, gives him a unique view of the world and is an asset in his writing. He began writing as a hobby while attending Grant MacEwan University to become a forensic analyst. Learning about his condition and exploring knowledge to improve his writing through Steve and Dani Alcorn's courses at Writing Academy has given Michael a new way of seeing how his difference can be used. While primarily focusing on fantasy, he has a short story published in an anthology with Writing Academy, Michael also explores romance and

MICHAEL MCGEE

slice of life stories in his work. In his free time, Michael enjoys skiing in the Canadian mountains and always enjoys hitting the golf course as long as there's beer and friends.

Manufactured by Amazon.ca
Acheson, AB